ALIAS™

CLOSE QUARTERS

A MICHAEL VAUGHN NOVEL

EMMA HARRISON

AN ORIGINAL PREQUEL NOVEL BASED ON THE
HIT TV SERIES CREATED BY J.J. ABRAMS

BANTAM BOOKS
NEW YORK ★ TORONTO ★ LONDON ★ SYDNEY ★ AUCKLAND

Alias: Close Quarters/A Michael Vaughn Novel

A Bantam Book / September 2003
Text and cover art copyright © 2003 by Touchstone Television

ISBN: 0-553-49403-1

Visit us on the Web! www.randomhouse.com

Published simultaneously in the United States and Canada

Bantam Books is an imprint of Random House Children's Books, a
division of Random House, Inc. BANTAM BOOKS and the rooster
colophon are registered trademarks of Random House, Inc.

PRINTED IN THE UNITED STATES OF AMERICA

OPM 10 9 8 7 6 5 4 3 2 1

Vaughn saw something flit across Marianna's face at that moment—anger, resentment—something dark. But it was gone so fast it was easy to believe he had imagined it. Perhaps she hated that all the focus was on her, being the president's only child.

"Well, I *am* glad you were there tonight," she told him, looking away again. "Thank you for that."

"Don't thank me," Vaughn said sincerely. "I only wish I had gotten there sooner."

Marianna smiled, and for the second time that night, they locked eyes. Vaughn felt his heart respond with a thump to her unabashed stare. He found himself dropping his gaze to her perfect, full lips—imagining what she might do if he just leaned forward and—

No! A little voice in his mind called out. He blinked, breaking eye contact, and stood up. *Don't go there,* he thought, wiping his palms against his thighs. *You cannot go there.*

"I'm starving. You want anything from room service?" he asked, crossing to the phone.

"No thanks," Marianna said. She reached for the remote and clicked on the TV. Vaughn felt his shoulders relax as a laugh track blared through the speakers. Just like that, the moment was over, the tension gone.

JUST DON'T LET IT HAPPEN AGAIN, HE TOLD HIM-SELF AS HE DIALED ROOM SERVICE. ROMANCE ON THE JOB IS NEVER A GOOD IDEA.

ALIAS™

CLOSE QUARTERS

1

MICHAEL VAUGHN WOULD NEVER have admitted it, but sometimes he still felt beyond cool when he walked into Central Intelligence Agency headquarters. He'd step across the CIA seal on the floor in the center of the lobby, his head held a bit higher than usual, a casual smile on his chiseled face, and think, *Check me out. I'm a CIA agent. Yeah, that's right, I'm a badass.*

Then he'd laugh at himself and try to keep a straight face until he got past security.

This wasn't CIA agent behavior, he knew. It wasn't even adult behavior. But he couldn't help it.

It had started back when he'd reported for training at the Farm. That first day it had hit him: He was finally fulfilling his lifelong dream to be one of the good guys, to protect the United States and its citizens from all threats, foreign or domestic. That day he'd gotten a sort of adrenaline-fueled thrill. And now, more than a year later, he still felt it. He was cool. James Bond cool. Han Solo cool. He was the guy every other guy wished he could be.

On this warm spring day, Vaughn was feeling his cool factor more intensely than usual. He and his new partner, Chloe Murphy, had just returned from a mission in the Middle East—a dangerous, confidential, top-priority mission—and they had returned home triumphant. Not only had they taken out a powerful terrorist cell, but they had secured two warehouses full of illegal weapons. This morning, Vaughn was feeling good. He was feeling like a hero.

Chloe had been one of his fellow trainees at the Farm. After his first partner, Akiko Schwartz, had opted for a desk job at the CIA's Center for Families, he'd been reassigned to team with Chloe, a baby-faced wunderkind with a Ph.D. in linguistics who'd just come back from a stint in Paris.

He nodded to Rufus and Tom, the two guards outside the secure room that led to the Outer Rim at

CIA headquarters. The Outer Rim was the nickname the agents had given to the long, white hallway that surrounded the offices of the CIA. Vaughn placed his palm on the handprint scanner in the secure room and waited as a beam of light illuminated his skin. His picture appeared on the security screen along with his clearance code and status: active.

"State your name," a female voice said, filling the small room.

"Michael Vaughn."

The voice-recognition computer beeped its approval. The glass door in front of Vaughn slid open, and he stepped into the Outer Rim. Brightly lit and deathly quiet, the Rim smelled of antiseptic cleaner that always reminded Vaughn of hospitals. He walked across the gleaming linoleum floor and stood before the door to the bullpen-style office within. As always, he strained not to blink as the red laser for the retinal scan slid over his eyeball. Finally the steel door before him unlocked, and Vaughn pushed his way inside.

The office, as always, was buzzing with activity. People rushed around carrying files, talking into headsets. Three senior agents huddled over a flat-screen monitor, urgently whispering over some new intel. Phones trilled and printers whined.

Vaughn headed for the far side of the room, where he and his fellow junior agents sat in a cluster of six desks, set up so that each agent faced his or her partner. Chloe was already at her desk, her long brown hair held back in a messy bun with two pencils. She sipped a huge cup of coffee, her eyes trained on her monitor.

"'Morning," Vaughn said, sliding into his leather chair.

Chloe glanced up and smiled, her hazel eyes glittering. "We are so money right now."

"Yeah? Everyone's heard?" Vaughn asked, leaning back and unbuttoning his suit jacket.

Chloe spotted someone over his shoulder and lifted her chin with a smile.

"Vaughn, my man!" Agent Chris Seale called out, holding up his hand to slap palms with Vaughn. Chris was a former Penn State linebacker—a guy whose body always seemed to be straining to break free from his pressed shirts and too-tight ties. Vaughn stood up to give him a high five, and Chris almost knocked him off his feet.

"It's all over the office," Chris said, sitting down at his desk next to Vaughn's, his huge form practically overflowing from the chair.

Vaughn scratched at the back of his scruffy light brown hair, grinning with pride. This was exactly how he'd pictured it all the way home on the long flight from Cairo to Paris to Boston to D.C. Back-slapping, congratulations, general adulation. He was sure his and Chloe's success in the Middle East was going to land them a prime assignment their next time out. Something even bigger, even more treacherous and significant. He couldn't wait to find out what it would be.

"Hey, Vaughn, Murphy. Betty wants to see you in her office," Jordan Patel, another of their peers, told them as he dropped into his own chair. He barely glanced at the other agents before firing up his computer. No "Welcome home." No "Good job." Not that Vaughn was surprised. Patel was one of those people who couldn't stand it when others succeeded—even if they were all on the same team.

Vaughn met Chloe's gaze as they stood up, and he could tell she was as excited as he was to talk to their boss. This was it. Betty was sure to reward their success with a fabulous assignment.

"What do you think it'll be?" Chloe asked under her breath as she fell into step next to Vaughn. They wound their way around the clusters of desks, acknowledging a few more congratulations as they went.

"I don't know," Vaughn told her, his heart pounding. "Russia . . . China . . . Indonesia . . . ?"

He held open the door to Betty Harlow's office for Chloe. As they stepped into the soundproof room, Betty reached for her cane, using it to help push herself up from her chair. Betty had been in charge of training at the Farm when Vaughn and Chloe were there learning the skills that would turn them into ace officers. Back then they had been petrified of her. They were still scared, in fact, but to a lesser degree. Betty reminded Vaughn of an aging folk singer, with long graying brown hair and a no-nonsense attitude. She was in charge, and everyone around her knew it by her very presence. But after everything Vaughn had been through with her, he'd grown to respect and admire her—even if that one heavy-lidded eye still appeared in his nightmares now and then.

"Nice work in the desert," Betty said, nodding to the visitors' chairs across from her.

"Thank you, ma'am," Vaughn and Chloe said in unison before perching on the edge of their seats.

Betty lowered herself into her chair again and passed them each a folder marked CONFIDENTIAL. Vaughn glanced at Chloe and felt his pulse speed up the way it always did the moment before they discovered what their next quest would be.

"I'm sending both of you to New York," Betty told them.

Good start, Vaughn said. New York wasn't

some exotic foreign locale, but as cities went, it wasn't too shabby. Vaughn focused on his boss and rested his file in his lap unopened. Betty hated it when they cracked their dockets before she told them to.

"As you well know, the annual UN conference is taking place this week, and dignitaries from all over the world will be descending on Manhattan," Betty continued. "The CIA will be sending dozens of teams to the city for added security and to cover special assignments. Your mission is as follows."

Betty hit a switch on her desk, and the lights in her office dimmed. A large plasma screen on the wall to Vaughn's left blinked to life, showing stock video of Ramero Toscana, the president of Italy, and his wife, Martina. On the screen, Toscana, a short, stocky man with thick salt-and-pepper hair and a permanent tan, waved to a crowd of cheering onlookers. His wife clutched his hand and pressed her other palm to her mouth, blowing kisses to the people before ducking into a limousine behind her husband. The Toscanas were, as always, impeccably dressed and coiffed, and exuded an air of health and well-being, as if they had just come from a relaxing spa day with an expert stylist.

"The Italian government has reported several threats to the life of President Ramero Toscana from a militant organization called La Rappre-saglia," Betty explained.

"The Retaliation," Vaughn translated easily. Fluent in Spanish and French, he had found it fairly simple to perfect yet another romance language.

"Very good," Betty said with a brief nod.

"Suck-up," Chloe joked under her breath. In Italian.

Vaughn felt his cheeks redden slightly. He had to work on resisting the impulse to blurt out a transla-tion when he was around Chloe, who was practically a United Nations unto herself—she knew Russian, Spanish, French, Chinese, and, obviously, Italian.

Betty continued. "The president and his family will be in New York for the next few days, and Toscana is scheduled to deliver the address at the closing ceremony of this year's conference."

Vaughn watched more stock footage of Toscana—delivering a speech, cutting a red ribbon in front of a new hospital. *Get to the good stuff,* he urged Betty silently. *What's the mission?*

"La Rappresaglia's latest threat is that they will assassinate the president while he is on U.S. soil," Betty said ominously.

Vaughn's heart seized slightly, and his gaze shifted from the video screen back to Betty. She turned to face him and Chloe, her eyes narrowing until the heavy-lidded right one was practically closed. "I don't have to tell you that if this were to happen, there would be major international repercussions. The consequences could be disastrous."

Swallowing hard, Vaughn looked at Chloe. Were they going to be sent after the assassins? Would they be protecting the president? What? He could see the headlines now: ASSASSINATION ATTEMPT THWARTED! Of course, his identity would have to be protected, so the newspapers wouldn't be able to mention his name, but still—

"Your assignment is to protect the president's daughter, Marianna Toscana," Betty said, hitting another button and facing the screen again. "She already has a personal bodyguard, but we want some of our own people on the job."

Vaughn's jaw dropped. *Huh?* He glanced at the monitor and saw some grainy, dated footage of Toscana with his arm around a teenage girl with unruly curls and a mouth full of braces. Vaughn suspected that the film had been shot at least a couple of years ago, but the girl couldn't have been much older than fifteen.

"Wait a minute. We're going to be *baby-sitting?*" Vaughn blurted out before his brain could check his mouth. Every now and then the whole think-before-you-speak concept still eluded him.

Chloe hunched forward and closed her eyes, shaking her head slightly. Vaughn knew what she was thinking—*Nice move, moron.*

"I wouldn't look at it that way, Agent Vaughn," Betty said, snapping the lights on again. The screen faded to black and she leaned forward over her desk. "Any threat to the president is considered a threat to his family. This is a matter of international security. Do you two find this country's concerns to be *beneath* you?"

"No, ma'am," Chloe piped up.

"No, ma'am," Vaughn echoed, his voice cracking slightly. Much to his chagrin, he found that his palms had grown sweaty. Unbelievable. Two weeks enduring the tension in the Middle East and he had been as calm as a frozen pond. Two minutes with Betty and he was reduced to mush.

"Good," Betty said. "And you won't be babysitting, Agent Vaughn. While you're in New York, you will be gathering intel, interviewing Ms. Toscana's personnel. If you open your dossiers, you will find that the Italian government has reason to believe that this faction has people on the inside—people who may have easy access to the first family."

Vaughn opened his file with less excitement and anticipation than he normally would have. All he could see in his mind's eye was that little awkward girl standing next to her father. One day he was taking out terrorists and the next he was going to be trapped with a teenybopper, listening to bubblegum pop CDs on automatic replay and braiding her hair. Not that he would ever actually *do* that.

"You'll have more time to review that information on the plane, which takes off in one hour," Betty told them, standing again. Vaughn and Chloe slapped their files shut and jumped to their feet. "I cannot stress this enough, you two: We cannot lose a member of the Italian first family."

"We won't," Vaughn said, imagining Patel gloating at the news of his rival's failure.

"Agent Vaughn, you will act as a second bodyguard to Marianna. Stay with her at all times. I don't care if she wants to drag you to the Ice Capades, you'll go," Betty told him firmly. Vaughn suddenly conjured up a new mental picture of himself in Madison Square Garden, holding a cone of pink cotton candy with a neon glow ring on his head while skaters twirled on the ice below.

Yeah. Han Solo cool, he thought morosely. *James Bond cool.*

"Agent Murphy, you'll be working behind the scenes, gathering intel, assessing any new threats. I'm sending Elena and Barry with you in case any special tech needs arise." Betty eyed them expectantly. "Any questions?"

Yeah. What happened to Indonesia? "No, ma'am," Vaughn said instead.

"Then get a move on," Betty told them.

Chloe and Vaughn strode out of the office and waited until they were a good ten yards away before speaking a word. They paused near the restrooms, looking warily across the office at their desks. Chris and Jordan appeared to be hard at work, but they would definitely be all over them about the new assignment the second they returned.

"I bet Chris is salivating to know what exciting adventures we'll be up to next," Chloe said, holding her file down in front of her with both hands.

"They find out what we're really doing and we are never going to live it down," Vaughn replied under his breath. "Jordan will milk this till Christmas."

"So we tell them it's highly classified and we're not allowed to divulge the details or we'll all be killed?" Chloe suggested, lifting a shoulder.

Vaughn caught Patel's inquiring gaze. "Every last one of us."

2

"I CAN'T IMAGINE WHAT SORT of special tech needs might arise on this mission," Barry said, sitting down in the cushy leather airplane seat next to Vaughn. "I mean, unless Vaughn wants us to speed-write an electronic dictionary of teen lingo so he can keep up with the girl."

Barry rubbed his slim, paler-than-pale hands together. The blue sky and fluffy white clouds were reflected in the thick lenses of his glasses. "A Betty is a babe, not Wilma's sidekick, and not our boss back at Langley. You know that, right?" Barry joked, snorting a laugh.

"Very funny," Vaughn said, trying not to let his wounded pride show. How uncool was it that Barry knew more current lingo than he did? He rested his chin on his hand and stared out the window at the billowing tops of the white clouds below. "I checked the file. Marianna Toscana just turned twenty-one. She's not a teenager anymore."

"Close enough," Barry said with a smile. Then he sniffed the air, leaned toward Vaughn, and sniffed again. "You changed deodorants, didn't you?"

Vaughn shot a desperate glance at Chloe, who sat across the aisle next to Elena. They had their heads bent together, looking over something on Elena's sleek laptop. Normally Vaughn found Barry's quirky sense of humor and even quirkier sense of smell somewhat amusing, but not today. Chloe didn't catch his plea, however, and Vaughn was temporarily trapped.

"You did! You smell completely different, my friend. The nose knows," Barry said, sniffing again. "You may as well tell me what it is—you know I'm going to figure it out."

"It's Degree," Vaughn told him flatly. "And I don't know why I'd want to keep it a secret."

"Well, some people are private about their personal antiperspirant preferences," Barry said, sitting back in his seat. His dark ponytail was forced out at an angle, hanging over his shoulder.

Vaughn leaned forward to see past Barry and glanced at Agent Mike Roscoe, one of the CIA's leading experts on Italy, who sat across the way, muttering into one of the plane's satellite telephones. From the sound of the conversation, he was slowly wrapping it up. Vaughn willed him to talk fast. Roscoe had been sent along to brief the team on the current situation in Italy, and Vaughn was more than ready to get the show on the road.

"Now . . . *flash* is a new word for *swag,* which is an old new word for any kind of ostentatious stuff that you wear or use to let your homeys know how rich you are," Barry continued, tugging down the sleeves of his ever-present black turtleneck. "You know, like diamonds, gold necklaces, furs, Hummers."

Mercifully, Roscoe hung up the phone and stood, clapping his hands together.

"All right, everyone, if I could have your attention, please," Roscoe said. He was a short man with wiry black hair and a broad weightlifter's build. Even at eleven o'clock in the morning he had a five o'clock shadow dotting his chin and neck. His loud voice boomed through the tiny airplane. Barry actually jumped when the man spoke.

Vaughn gave Roscoe his full attention, and Elena and Chloe closed the laptop. Roscoe popped open the black briefcase that rested on the seat across from his and started to pull out documents and photos.

"Unfortunately, we don't know much about La Rappresaglia," Roscoe told them, handing each agent a packet of papers. "What we do know is that they've taken credit for a long list of crimes that have taken place in Italy in recent months. Everything ranging from the murder of Tomas Impenniolla, President Toscana's top domestic policy advisor, to the smash-and-grab job at the Cartier store in Rome. They took both jewels and cash and sold the more precious items on the black market, presumably to fund their little enterprise."

Vaughn flipped through his packet and paused at the pictures of the Impenniolla crime scene. The body lay facedown in a driveway in front of a vine-covered villa. There seemed to be blood everywhere, soaking the man's shirt, spreading out around his body. In one of the photographs, police officers were marking off the crime scene, but there were a few spectators looking on. A little girl with blond curls stood in front of a woman who was clearly her mother, and both were hysterically crying, mouths open in silent wails. For some reason,

Vaughn couldn't tear his eyes away from that little girl.

"Impenniolla was gunned down in front of his family at their vacation home outside Naples," Roscoe said, noticing the page Vaughn held on his lap. "These people are ruthless, and they are damn good at keeping their identities secret. We could be dealing with a force of anywhere from ten people to a hundred."

Vaughn swallowed hard and finally closed his packet over that terrified little face. He knew firsthand what it was like to lose a father as a child—his own father, a CIA agent, had been killed in the line of duty when Vaughn was just a boy, and not a day passed that he didn't think of him and of what was lost. But to see it happen—to have a parent brutally murdered right before your eyes . . . Vaughn was certain he would never have recovered from that.

"These people are monsters," Elena said, her dark eyes horrified behind her black-rimmed glasses.

Vaughn couldn't have agreed more.

"That's why we have to take them down," Roscoe said, loosening his tie slightly. "While we're in New York, we have to do everything possible to find any members of this faction and bring them in. These people made a big mistake coming to the U.S. Let's make sure they go back to Italy in cuffs."

Vaughn looked up at Roscoe and locked eyes with him. He nodded his assent, determined. He would do whatever it took to protect Marianna Toscana from these bastards. If anyone tried anything, they were going down.

He opened his packet again and got to work, studying every last detail the pages provided. As he read, he felt his pre-mission adrenaline rush start to kick in and smiled, welcoming the familiar sensation. Maybe this wasn't such a lame mission after all.

* * *

In the plushly carpeted hallway outside President Toscana's suite at the Plaza Hotel in New York City, Vaughn stood against the wall alongside Chloe, Barry, and Elena. He felt like a first grader lining up before being walked to gym class. Only now he was nervous. He'd never been nervous about PE in his life.

"What do you think they're like?" Chloe whispered, eyeing the two impossibly large Italian secret service men who stood on either side of the door. Agent Roscoe was inside at the moment, talking to the first family and briefing them on the security detail the CIA was providing for Marianna.

"From everything I've heard, Toscana is a good man," Vaughn replied. "He started out as a local politician and worked his way up through the ranks."

"So why do these La Rappresaglia people hate him so much?" Chloe asked, smoothing her hair down behind her ears—her only nervous tic, as far as Vaughn had observed.

"It can be tough to explain the motivations of psychotics," Vaughn replied. The moment the words were out of his mouth, the door to the suite opened, and his heart skipped a beat.

Agent Roscoe stuck his head out into the hallway. "We're ready for you."

He opened the door a bit wider and a loud female voice blasted into the hallway, screeching in Italian. The woman was speaking too fast for Vaughn to understand it all, but she was saying something like, "How could you do this to me? Why do you hate me?"

Vaughn and Chloe exchanged a wary glance. "You sure?" Chloe asked Agent Roscoe. "They don't sound ready."

"She'll adjust," Roscoe told them. Then his brow furrowed. "Hopefully."

Great. Just what I need, Vaughn thought as he entered the room with the rest of the team. President Toscana and his wife stood near the windows across the living area, clearly pleading with their daughter. The moment they saw the agents walk in, a young woman Vaughn recognized as Marianna narrowed her eyes and stormed over to the nearest couch.

The first daughter had definitely outgrown the awkward phase she'd been struggling with in the video Betty had shown them. Gone were the braces and unruly curls, replaced with gleaming white teeth and shoulder-skimming sleek black hair. She wore a pair of form-fitting jeans, black leather boots, and a black cashmere sweater. Diamonds sparkled in her ears. She sat, crossed her legs at the knee and her arms over her chest, and slumped down.

"Non sono una bambina," she said under her breath, pouting.

Oh, no, you're not a baby, Vaughn thought sarcastically.

President Toscana and his wife rearranged their distressed expressions into warm smiles and walked over to greet the team.

"Mr. President, Mrs. Toscana," Roscoe said, nodding. "These are our tech specialists, Elena and Barry. This is Agent Chloe Murphy, who will be working point. And this is Agent Michael Vaughn, who will be assisting Marianna's personal security detail."

"It's a pleasure to meet you," President Toscana said, shaking their hands. "I can't thank you enough for your concern for my daughter's safety."

"It's an honor to meet you, sir," Vaughn said sincerely, noting the president's firm grip. "I think I speak for the team when I say that we will do everything in our power to make sure Marianna is protected."

"Thank you," President Toscana said with a slight bow.

"I apologize for Marianna's rudeness," Mrs. Toscana added in a lilt Vaughn recognized as Milanese. She lifted her chin and shot a reprimanding glance at her daughter. "She does not take well to authority."

"Who does?" Chloe joked, trying to lighten the mood.

The president and his wife chuckled, and Vaughn cracked a smile. He turned to look at Marianna, determined to make some kind of inroad with her. She looked up at him and blinked, her dark eyes narrowing slightly.

"Wait a minute," she said in perfect English. "*He's* my new baby-sitter?"

"I wouldn't put it that way," Vaughn said politely, with a deferential smile. *So she's on to her parents' plan too.*

Marianna stood up. "I had no idea Americans could be so hot," she said after a moment's pause, looking him up and down with what could only be called a leer.

"Marianna!" Mrs. Toscana scolded, paling.

Vaughn managed an embarrassed laugh. "Thanks. I think." Then, feeling every pair of eyes in the room boring into him, he cleared his throat and headed for safer ground. "Ms. Toscana, I assure you that the CIA is dedicated to ensuring your stay in New York is a safe one," he said, all business.

Agent Roscoe stepped in and gave the Italian first family a rundown of the security detail and what they could expect from Vaughn and Chloe.

Marianna's smile widened as she stepped closer to Vaughn—so close he could smell her perfume. He knew she was messing with him just to annoy her parents, and he stood as still as possible, gazing right back into her dark eyes, refusing to let her get the better of him. But inside he was growing more and more irritated. Clearly this girl did not understand the gravity of her situation. Hadn't she seen the footage of the Impenniolla murder? Didn't she understand that these people were serious?

"So . . . you have to go wherever I go, right?" Marianna asked, tilting her head back to look up at him.

"That's my assignment, yes," Vaughn said, hands clasped behind his back.

"Fabulous," Marianna said. To Vaughn's relief, she turned and walked across the room, freeing him from the torture of scrutiny and the heady feeling her perfume had brought on. She grabbed a purse from the coffee table, picked up a cream-colored suede jacket, and stalked across the room to the door. One of the bodyguards who stood along the wall stepped up next to her. He was a large, solid-looking guy with huge jowls and a frown that appeared permanent.

"Follow me," Marianna said to Vaughn.

Vaughn shot a glance at Roscoe, who pressed his lips together and shrugged in a "What can I do?" gesture.

"It was a pleasure meeting you," Vaughn told the president and first lady. "I'm sure I'll be seeing you again."

"Thank you, Agent Vaughn," the president said, shaking Vaughn's hand again. Then he lowered his voice and drew Vaughn a bit closer to him. "Good luck," he added.

Vaughn attempted a smile, but his stomach

shriveled. Great. Even her father thought a little luck was in order.

"Agent Vaughn . . . Michael . . . can I call you Mikey?" Marianna asked, arching her eyebrows as he approached.

"Agent Vaughn would be fine," he replied.

"Okay, Mikey," Marianna said with a mischievous grin. "This is my bodyguard, Dominic Rizzio." She slapped her hand against the frowning man's chest. "You two may as well get to know each other. You're going to be spending *a lot* of time together."

Vaughn held his hand out to Dominic to shake, but Dominic just stared him down with disgust and followed Marianna out of the room. Vaughn reddened and turned to look at Chloe. She smiled and discreetly flashed him a sarcastic thumbs-up, her back to the president and his wife.

Vaughn took a deep breath and followed his charge and her surly companion. Suddenly he had a feeling this was going to be a very long day.

3

"MIKEY, WOULD YOU SAY you're more into red lace or basic black?"

Vaughn stood in the entrance to the Victoria's Secret dressing room and rolled his eyes at the closed door Marianna was changing behind. She'd been trying to irritate him, embarrass him, and otherwise harass him all day, but the really annoying thing was that she wasn't even attempting to be coy about it. For a woman who had attended some of the finest schools in the world, she definitely hadn't learned the art of subtlety.

"I would bet you are a basic black person," she

said. Vaughn could see her feet moving under the bottom of the door as she stepped in and out of various items of clothing. "You don't seem like the adventurous type."

Yeah. If you could have seen what I was doing last week at this time, you wouldn't say that, Vaughn thought. He had never thought any experience could make him long for the desert fatigues and foxholes he'd found himself in back in the Middle East, but this shopping excursion was getting him there.

Vaughn sighed and looked around the store. None of the other dressing rooms was occupied, but the store was packed with shoppers—not the most secure environment. Vaughn had suggested that they call ahead and ask the store to close for an hour—they did that for famous people, didn't they? But Marianna would have none of it. She wanted to be part of "reality," as she said, traipsing down the streets of Soho and the Village seemingly oblivious to the curious stares of passers-by.

"Does your bodyguard make a habit of disappearing and leaving you alone in crowded shops?" Vaughn asked through the door.

"Dominic just went outside for a smoke," Marianna called over the sounds of hangers rattling. "I believe he's a bit offended by your presence."

"Really? I hadn't noticed," Vaughn said flatly.

Dominic had, in fact, been giving Vaughn the silent treatment all morning—unless grunts, groans, and actual growls counted as communication. As Marianna dragged them to store after store on Fifth Avenue, gradually winding her way downtown to this lingerie store, which Vaughn hoped would be the last stop, Dominic had spurned every one of Vaughn's attempts at conversation. Finally, somewhere between Chanel and Tocca, Vaughn had given up.

He eyed the dozens of colorful packages at his feet. Marianna had refused to leave a single item in the limo—just in case she wanted to try something on over the lingerie. Vaughn had spent fifteen minutes carrying it all inside while Dominic sat in the front seat of the limo, chatting in Italian on his cell phone. It wasn't until Vaughn had finished the transfer that Dominic had finally come inside. He'd hung out for two minutes, ogling mannequins and fingering a few silk slips before he'd disappeared.

"So, Vaughn, what did you do today?" Vaughn imagined Chloe asking when he returned to the *hotel.*

"Well, I trained as a personal shopper and *a lackey,"* Vaughn heard himself reply.

He sighed again and shook his head, rubbing

his brow between his thumb and forefinger. His brain started to list places he'd much rather be: on the ice playing hockey, on the phone catching up with Akiko, going for a nice long run. Hell, he'd rather be playing Scrabble. As long as it wasn't with Elena or Barry, both of whom he was sure could kick his butt at any board game.

"Are you almost done in there?" he asked, finally letting his impatience show.

"Only a few more things to try on, Mikey," Marianna said. He heard the lock on the door click and glanced up as it opened. Vaughn felt his face start to flush and did his best to control it. Marianna was standing there in a lavender nightie that barely covered the tops of her thighs. Her curls tumbled over her face, sexily covering one eye. She raised the visible eyebrow at him, leaning against the doorframe in a sultry pose.

"What do you think of this?" Marianna asked, her full lips twisting into a playful smirk. "Purple has always been my color."

Vaughn averted his eyes, making a show of inspecting the store. "Like you said, I'm a basic black man," he lied. In truth, Marianna could have just stepped out of the Victoria's Secret catalog itself. She looked that amazing.

Too bad she's a brat, Vaughn thought.

He heard the dressing room door slam and took a deep breath. He ran another mental check of the customers in the store. There was the mother-daughter combo on the far side, looking over long, white nightgowns. A couple of teenagers hovered by the thongs, giggling and blushing and looking around furtively. Vaughn had a hunch they were shoplifting, but he let it go. He had bigger criminals to deal with.

The young couple who had started out by the cotton pajamas was now inspecting some freaky-looking bustier-type things in the back of the store. A few other shoppers Vaughn had noticed before were lined up at the register. Everything appeared to be in order.

Then Vaughn saw something move out of the corner of his eye. He turned and spotted a pair of middle-aged men hovering near one of the perfume displays. That was odd. In general men didn't step into a store like this unless they had the buffer of a woman to deflect embarrassing questions from the salespeople. Every once in a while a braver guy would venture in to buy something for his wife or girlfriend, but they generally got in and out as quickly as possible. It was mid-March—too late for Valentine's Day shopping, too early for Mother's Day. So what were these two men doing here?

"You about ready?" Vaughn asked Marianna, keeping his voice casual so as not to alarm her.

"Patience, Mikey. Sheesh. Haven't you ever had a girlfriend?" she replied.

"My personal life is not your concern," he said, a bit too forcefully. Ever since he'd drifted apart from his college girlfriend, Nora, Vaughn had pretty much written women off. Not that he didn't want someone special. It just . . . well, it just wasn't happening.

One of the men looked up, directly at Vaughn, and he felt the little hairs on the back of his neck stand on end. The two men parted, and one headed for the back corner of the store, out of Vaughn's line of sight.

"All right then, don't move," Vaughn said. "No matter what, just stay in the dressing room."

"Fine by me," Marianna replied. "Going somewhere?"

"Just stay put," Vaughn said tersely. He wanted to get that second guy back in view.

Slowly, trying to look like just another bored boyfriend, Vaughn moved away from the dressing room, always keeping one eye on the door. He walked to the center of the shop and saw the second guy talking with a saleswoman. The first man still hovered near the perfumes, absently looking through rows of bottles. He didn't seem remotely interested in what he was doing.

These two are up to something. I can feel it, Vaughn thought. He glanced around the room for Dominic, hoping the only person who could possibly be called in for backup had finally decided to do his job, but the guy was nowhere to be found.

Vaughn pressed his lips together and tried to keep his frustration in check. It wasn't easy. What was wrong with these people? Didn't they comprehend the seriousness of the threat they were dealing with?

A loud crash behind Vaughn sent him whirling around, hand under his jacket, reaching for his gun. But his alarm was unfounded. The first shady man had simply knocked over about twenty glass bottles of perfume. A couple of saleswomen were instantly on the scene, helping the embarrassed, fumbling guy straighten the mess. Vaughn turned around again to check on the guy's friend—and he was gone.

Vaughn's body temperature skyrocketed as he scanned the store, but the man was gone. He spun back toward the dressing room.

"Marianna?" Vaughn said, arriving at the door.

Nothing. Vaughn swallowed hard and looked at the space beneath the door to her room. No feet. No movement.

A customer clasping a bunch of bras entered the hallway. "Closed," Vaughn said brusquely, motioning the confused woman out.

"Marianna? Are you still in there?" Vaughn asked.

Please tell me I didn't just mess up the easiest assignment in history, he thought, pulling his gun out. He held it in front of him with both hands, his pulse pounding in his ears. Reaching up with his right leg, he smashed the door to the dressing room in with one swift thrust.

Marianna sat on a plush pink bench, in a corner a safe distance from the splintered door, fully clothed. She took one look at Vaughn's distressed expression and began to laugh.

Vaughn lowered his gun, feeling more murderous than he ever had in his life. "Why didn't you answer me?"

"You should *see* the look on your face right now," Marianna said through her laughter. Then she turned and looked in the full-length mirror behind her. "Oh, wait, you *can*."

Vaughn turned away without checking his reflection. He wouldn't give her the satisfaction. "Get your stuff together," he said, his heart rate starting to return to normal. "We're going back to the hotel."

"Yes, Mikey," Marianna said with a smile, slipping into her suede jacket.

After Vaughn discreetly explained the broken dressing room door to the store manager, he escorted Marianna back to the limo.

"What the hell did you think you were doing in there?" Vaughn demanded as he tossed her bags into the trunk. He slammed it so hard the entire vehicle bounced up and down on its tires.

"Just a little fun," Marianna told him, raising her small shoulders.

"This is not a game," Vaughn said through his teeth, getting as in-her-face as he dared. "Don't you understand that your life is at stake? How stupid can you be?"

Marianna's eyes seemed to darken as she glared up at him. "No one speaks to me that way," she snapped. "You had better watch what you say, Mikey. My father can have you fired in an instant."

Vaughn glared back at her, a million retorts flying through his head. He sincerely doubted that the American government would fire him over a spat with the most spoiled princess of the millennium, but he decided to keep his mouth shut. He could be the bigger person here. He had to be. Marianna was clearly incapable of taking the high road.

It's just a few days, he told himself. *You just have to get through the next few days.*

He popped open the back door to the limousine, the scents of leather and new car wafting onto the street. Marianna narrowed her eyes at him, then slipped into the car, depositing herself in the center of the backseat. Vaughn slammed the door a little harder than necessary, half wishing her foot were in the way.

At that moment, Dominic emerged from around the side of the building, talking into his cell phone. He closed it when he saw Vaughn eyeing him and walked over to the driver's side door without a word.

"Where were you?" Vaughn demanded over the roof of the car.

"You are not my boss, American," Dominic shot back. He got into the car and started revving the engine, threatening to peel out and leave Vaughn standing on the sidewalk.

Great level of cooperation we've got going here, Vaughn thought, ripping the door open. He felt as if his head were about to explode from dealing with these people. Had Dominic just been chatting on his phone the entire time he and Marianna had been in the store? How could anyone assigned to the first family possibly be so careless?

As Dominic pulled the car into traffic on Broadway, Vaughn settled into his seat, thinking back over everything that had just happened. The two men in the store were most likely not suspects—they were a little too clumsy for La Rappresaglia—but he'd give Chloe full descriptions just to be safe. The thing that bothered him most of all was Dominic's behavior. He'd hung up the phone too fast upon seeing Vaughn, and for a moment he'd looked like a deer caught in headlights. Who had he been talking to? Roscoe had mentioned that there could be faction members working on the inside of the president's detail. Was Dominic one of them?

Vaughn checked the man out surreptitiously. A scowl was fixed on his face as he negotiated the busy Manhattan streets, his arms tense as he gripped the wheel.

Something was up with Dominic.

Vaughn was going to make it his business to find out what it was.

4

"I CAN'T BELIEVE YOU didn't pick me up anything." Chloe dipped a few french fries in a glob of ketchup. Vaughn had just finished telling her and Elena the tale of his exciting, high-risk day o' shopping over a room-service order of burgers and fries.

While Vaughn had been out running around the city, the rest of the team had set up a mini HQ in one of the hotel suites. The desks had been cleared to make way for scanners and fax machines and seventeen-inch monitors. A bulletin board against one wall was rapidly filling with information about La Rappresaglia, the president's itineraries, and other scraps of intel that were coming in over the wire. The TV in the corner was tuned to CNN's coverage of the UN conference, the volume turned down so that it could just be heard over the conversation at the table.

"A purse? A sweater?" Chloe munched away. "I'm not picky."

Vaughn unbuttoned his cuffs and rolled up his sleeves before digging into his food. "She actually modeled lingerie for me."

Elena dropped her fork. Two circles of pink appeared on Chloe's milky-white cheeks.

"See anything you like, Vaughn?" Elena asked, raising her eyebrows suggestively.

Vaughn blushed and bit into his burger. "Yeah, right. I'm a professional."

"Yeah. *And* a guy, last time I checked," Chloe said.

"A single guy," Elena added, stabbing another fry.

"Did you people not listen to a word I said?" Vaughn asked. "The girl's a little—"

"Watch it," Chloe warned, anticipating what he was intending to say. She raised a scolding finger in Vaughn's direction. Chloe didn't appreciate *language*.

"Well, you know what I mean," Vaughn finished.

"All right, let's get down to business," Chloe

said. A lock of hair fell free from her messy bun and she pushed it behind her ear before reaching for another fry. "Tell me more about Dominic. He sounds shady."

"My thoughts exactly," Vaughn told her. "He was with us all day, but when we got to the lingerie place he just disappeared. He was gone for at least an hour, and I think he was making phone calls the whole time."

"Not exactly the guy you want looking after your daughter," Chloe said.

"So, can we get a satellite tap on the phone?" Vaughn asked.

"Tried it," Chloe said, shaking her head. "His signal's blocked."

"That doesn't bode well," Vaughn said.

"Ooh! I just designed a new cell-phone tap! You're gonna love it!" Elena announced, jumping up from her seat. The woman never got excited about anything other than new technology. That and her arguments with Barry over which of them was the more dedicated technophile.

Chloe and Vaughn exchanged a smile as Elena rummaged through her stuff, knocking over a stack of disks in the process and banging her head against the side of a table. When she returned, she held a translucent disk about the size of a nickel between her thumb and forefinger.

"Careful," she said, holding it across the table toward Vaughn. He wiped his fingers on his linen napkin and took the disk from her. It looked like a plain piece of plastic until he turned it over, revealing intricate circuitry.

"All you have to do is get hold of his cell phone, slide the cartridge out, and place that over the central circuits. It'll attach like Velcro, and we'll be able to hear everything that's said."

Vaughn smiled up at her. "You're good, Elena."

"I know," she said, preening. She handed him a little black felt pouch. "Keep it in there until you're ready to use it."

"Thanks," Vaughn said. He placed the disk in the pouch and, lifting his jacket off the back of the chair next to his, slid it into the breast pocket.

"Where's Barry, anyway? I figured he'd smell this food from a mile away," Vaughn asked, taking another bite of his burger.

"He got a day off to visit with his brother. Tommy's with the NYPD, so Barry went to walk the beat with him," Elena said, clearly amused.

Vaughn smirked. He could just imagine Barry out on the streets, flinching at every shout and diving behind his brother whenever a car backfired. "We're in for some interesting stories."

"*We* are, anyway," Elena said. "*You'll* be out with your personal lingerie model tonight."

"Don't remind me," Vaughn said with a groan.

"Think you'll have an opportunity to get your hands on Dominic's phone?" Chloe asked.

"Probably. Marianna's dragging us both to some club downtown tonight," Vaughn told them, grimacing. "A gathering of young dignitaries."

Chloe and Elena laughed, exchanging a knowing glance.

"What?" Vaughn asked.

"I'd kill to see you on a dance floor," Chloe said, tipping her head back slightly, as if she were asking God to grant her the favor of catching Vaughn in *Dance Fever* mode.

Vaughn turned crimson, suddenly recalling a hundred high school humiliations. Slow dancing he could do. Anything with a beat—the results were not pretty. "That is one thing neither you nor Marianna will *ever* see."

* * *

Trick was the Manhattan club of the moment. Small and cramped, with more space for private VIP rooms than tables for everyday joes, it was the hot spot everyone wanted to experience. Thus the line of at least a hundred people standing outside in the rain, hoping to be noticed by the bouncers and granted entry. But Michael Vaughn had walked right by the crowd with Marianna and her entourage of friends and bodyguards. For tonight, he was one of the chosen ones—one of the beautiful, blessed people who were actually given access to this mecca of nightlife.

He couldn't have been less impressed.

The place was decorated like a hundred other bars in the city—black walls, red and purple faux-suede couches, random pillows in a thousand funky patterns. The low black tables that the sofas surrounded were chipped down to their original wood in various places. The tiled floor was covered with crushed cigarette butts and spilled drinks. There was nothing new.

Standing against the wall in the small cove Marianna had reserved for herself and a dozen of her children-of-dignitary friends, Vaughn felt as if he'd seen this exact spectacle countless times before. Different bar, same scene. Overprivileged kids getting drunk and stoned on Mommy and Daddy's money. Two-hundred-dollar bottles of champagne being passed around as if they held cheap beer. Smoke filled his lungs and stung his eyes as he kept watch over Marianna, who was, for the moment anyway, completely ignoring him—a shift that was more than fine by Vaughn.

Marianna sat on one of the velvet-covered stools that surrounded a table covered by half-empty glasses and overflowing ashtrays. She wore a pair of low-riding black leather pants and a silver halter that was no more than a handkerchief with string for straps. Every so often she would laugh at one of her friends' jokes, tossing her head back and exposing even more skin to the world. Every set of male eyes, and more than a few jealous female eyes, was drawn to her.

"What is with Mr. Stoic?" one of Marianna's friends asked in English, leaning toward her. The girl's straight blond hair was streaked with pink, and her eyes were bloodshot. From the lack of meat on her skinny frame and the obviousness of her collarbone, Vaughn figured she was either a heroin addict or an anorexic. Maybe both.

Vaughn knew the girl was referring to him, and he knew she'd intended for him to hear her. It was the first thing she'd said in English all night, and she'd said it loudly enough to be heard over the near-deafening music.

"Born with a stick up his butt," Marianna

replied, sipping at her apple martini. "All Americans were, you know. They act like they're such free spirits, but really it's a country full of repressed humanity." She looked Vaughn up and down, and he stared right back at her, refusing to look away and let her think she was embarrassing him. This was a childish game, and he hoped his expression conveyed his distaste. "Just look at him," Marianna continued. "No man that hot should be allowed to be so uptight."

Vaughn flushed but still didn't avert his gaze. It was dark enough in the room to hide the sudden color shift of his skin. At least Trick had that going for it.

Bored by his lack of response, Marianna and her friends went back to their conversation in Italian, and Vaughn continued to scan the club for suspicious-looking characters. Unfortunately, everyone in the place looked suspect. He glanced over at the bar and saw a tall man with a frizzy, light-brown ponytail sipping a glass of vodka as he checked out the scene. The man was dressed in black from head to toe, including an ill-fitting pair of leather pants. He raised his drink to his mouth to take a sip and Vaughn noticed a small, X-shaped scar on the left side of his chin. Next to him was a middle-aged blond guy, totally out of his element, talking with a beautiful brunette in a sexy but tasteful black dress. She wore tortoiseshell-framed glasses, and her lips were slick with gloss. And her body rocked. She was flirting, touching the man's arm and gazing up into his eyes, but the blond guy was barely paying attention. Instead, he gazed toward the other end of the bar, never cracking a smile.

Vaughn looked at the young woman again, watching as she tucked a strand of her bobbed hair behind her ear. What was wrong with that guy? If she'd chosen to flirt with Vaughn, he might actually have forgotten he was on assignment.

Which you are, lover boy, he reminded himself. He tore his eyes away from the couple and followed Mr. Blond's gaze toward the other end of the bar.

Dominic stood there with at least six other bodyguards knocking back shots and slapping one another on the back. A bitter taste filled Vaughn's mouth at the sight of such irresponsibility. This place was full of wealthy, important people from around the world—it was a prime target for kidnappers and terrorists. Yet the men who were paid to protect these kids were busy getting sloshed at the bar.

All the better for me, Vaughn thought, sensing his window. He leaned away from the wall, told Marianna, who ignored him, that he'd be right back, and made his way out of the private alcove and into the bar area. As he approached Dominic and his friends, the hulking man pushed away from the bar and spread his arms, smiling for the first time since Vaughn had met him.

"Agent Vaughn!" he bellowed at the top of his lungs, obliterating any cover Vaughn may have hoped to maintain. "Join us for a drink."

Wow. This guy really is *trashed,* Vaughn thought.

"Sure," Vaughn said, accepting Dominic's invitation. The sea of bodyguards parted slightly so that Vaughn and Dominic could lean on the bar. Dominic couldn't have made it any easier for Vaughn. As he reached up to try to get the bartender's attention, Vaughn slipped Dominic's cell phone from his pants pocket and deposited it in his own.

"Get me a scotch. I gotta hit the bathroom," Vaughn said.

"Little man can't hold his liquor!" Dominic said with a laugh, slapping Vaughn on the back.

Vaughn laughed in response and dove back through the crowd, heading in the direction of the bathrooms. He closed himself into a stall, slipped the cartridge from Dominic's phone, and placed Elena's disk over the central circuitry, pressing it down to make sure it was secure.

We'll see what this guy is really up to now, he

thought, putting the phone back together. He placed it back in his pocket, flushed the toilet for good measure, and headed back to the bar. Mr. Blond and his woman were headed for the door, and Vaughn let out a sigh of relief. One less person to watch.

"Here is your scotch!" Dominic said, handing Vaughn a tumbler full of alcohol he had no intention of drinking. "We toast your health!"

Each of the hulking bodyguards held up a drink and shouted, *"Salut!"* Vaughn took a sip of his drink to appease them as they each opened their mouths and gulped the full contents of their glasses down. A pair of drunken girls jostled into Vaughn on their way to the restrooms, and Vaughn made a big show of being thrown into Dominic's side so that he could transfer the phone again. He placed it back in the pocket he'd taken it from just before Dominic pushed him upright again.

"You shouldn't have any more," Dominic said, laughing as he took Vaughn's drink away. "You are a lightweight, my friend!"

Vaughn nodded and smiled. "You're right, you're right. I should get back to the table anyway."

He started to move away but paused when he saw Marianna walking out of the private cove with two young men. They each held one of her arms as they led her down the steps to the dance floor in the next room. One of the men was slim but powerful-looking, with cut arms and a goatee. The other man, taller, broader, and with more facial hair, laughed when Marianna missed a step and tripped into him. Something about these guys put Vaughn on alert.

"Dominic, who are those men with Marianna on the dance floor?" he asked as the trio joined the gyrating throng.

"Oh, they are just Carlos and Roberto Vianna," Dominic scoffed. "Carlos is the tall one and Roberto is the other. The CIA did not have you study up on Marianna's close friends?"

"They're friends?" Vaughn asked skeptically. Marianna didn't look entirely comfortable being jostled between the two men. And besides, if La Rappresaglia had people on the inside, they didn't necessarily have to be people that *worked* for the family—trusted friends were a possibility as well.

"The families go way back. Carlos and Roberto are cousins, and their parents visit the president and his family every summer on the Riviera," Dominic said lightly. "They grew up together. If you were not such an outsider, you would know this."

Vaughn ignored the dig and watched Marianna closely. She laughed as Roberto whispered something in her ear, but it was a strained laugh. Vaughn could tell something was up.

"Relax! She is fine!" Dominic said, slapping Vaughn on the shoulder.

Just then, Carlos and Roberto each grabbed one of Marianna's arms, more forcefully this time, and started to move toward the other side of the dance floor. Vaughn saw Marianna's eyes go wide before they turned her around, and then all he could see was her back as she struggled to free herself from their grip.

Heart in his throat, Vaughn jumped into action. He shoved his way through the mob by the bar, stepping on a few feet and causing more than one shout of protest. At the top of the stairs he could see the Viannas shoving Marianna toward a nearly hidden door on the other side of the dance floor. Vaughn scrambled down the steps, knowing that once he was at eye level with the dancing multitudes, he would lose sight of her for at least a minute.

As soon as he hit the dance floor, Vaughn made the snap decision to travel along the wall, taking the longer route. It would probably be faster than trying to cut through the tightly knit partyers in front of him. He moved as fast as he could, heading for the door he'd seen from above, hoping he wasn't too late.

Sidestepping a couple of lovers who were mauling each other next to the exit, Vaughn reached into his jacket and placed his hand on the butt of his gun, just in case. Then he turned to the side and slammed through the door.

The pelting rain hit Vaughn's face, and the first thing he heard was Marianna's scream. Vaughn withdrew his weapon and whirled to the left. What he saw made his blood run cold. Carlos had Marianna pressed up against the wall, his face buried in her neck. She looked at Vaughn, her makeup running down her face from the rain, her eyes terrified. This guy wasn't trying to assassinate Marianna, he was trying to rape her.

"Get away from her!" Vaughn shouted, aiming his gun at Carlos's head. He had to blink rapidly to clear the raindrops that were gathering around his eyelashes.

"Michael!" Marianna shouted.

Instinctively, Vaughn ducked, and Roberto came flying into view, having lost his balance from the momentum of his missed blow to Vaughn's head. He righted himself quickly and threw a right hook, which Vaughn easily blocked. He backhanded Roberto with his gun, then spun around and landed a roundhouse kick directly to his jaw. There was a loud *crack* before Roberto went down, knocking his head on the rain-slicked concrete.

"Roberto!" Carlos shouted, finally releasing Marianna. She slid to the ground, hugging her knees, as Carlos advanced on Vaughn. Once again, Vaughn trained his weapon on Carlos's chest.

"I wouldn't take another step if I were you," he said.

Carlos stopped and raised his hands in the air, swallowing hard. His thin white shirt was plastered to his heaving chest as he stared at the barrel of the gun.

"Up against the wall," Vaughn said, gesturing with his gun. Carlos did as he was told, and Vaughn pulled out his handcuffs and secured the man's hands behind his back. "You can have a seat," Vaughn said. His gun still trained on Carlos, he whipped out his cell phone, called Chloe, and told her to alert the NYPD.

Vaughn glanced down at Marianna's form against the wall and felt himself soften toward her slightly. She looked very wet, very small, and very scared.

"You all right?" he asked, standing over her.

Marianna nodded slowly, her eyes locking with his. She was still petrified, but also grateful. Vaughn smiled reassuringly as they heard sirens wail down the street. Maybe from now on, Marianna would trust him.

5

VAUGHN WALKED INTO MARIANNA'S hotel
room, leaving her outside with two of her father's
security men, and performed a quick sweep of
the room. He checked closets and looked behind
curtains and under beds until he was certain
the space was secure. When he opened the door
to tell Marianna to come in, she was leaning
against the wall, chin tucked, Vaughn's trench coat
pulled tightly around her small frame. They had
already been to see her extremely concerned
parents, and Marianna had put on a great act for
them, telling them she was fine and Vaughn had

protected her. She'd basically laughed the whole thing off.

But now, seeing her all withered and broken, Vaughn realized that what had happened had affected her more than she'd let on.

For the second time that night, Vaughn's heart went out to her.

"It's all clear. You can come in," he told her, stepping back.

Marianna lifted her head, shaking her damp curls back, and slipped into the room. She walked into the center of the thick pink carpet and paused, staring off toward the window.

"Are you okay?" Vaughn asked gently, keeping a safe distance from Marianna. She looked coiled, like she might lash out if anyone got too close.

"I'll be fine," she said finally. "I think I just need to get out of these clothes."

She handed Vaughn his jacket, crossed over to the large dresser against the wall, and pulled out a few things. Then she trudged slowly over to the bathroom and paused in front of the door.

"Where's Dominic?" she asked over her shoulder.

"Your father sent for him," Vaughn told her.

"He's in for a tongue-lashing he'll never forget," Marianna said with a sigh. She turned to look at Vaughn, her brown eyes uncertain. Her nose was red from crying, and her makeup was still smudged and smeared. "Do you think . . . would you mind staying for a little while?"

Vaughn swallowed. He definitely had a soft spot for vulnerable women. That was something Betty would tell him to work on if she knew. A CIA agent couldn't have any such weaknesses—it would make him too easy to manipulate. But that didn't mean he couldn't hang out until Marianna was comfortable enough to go to sleep. After all, watching over her was his job.

"Sure," he said with a small smile. "I'll be right here."

Marianna smiled in return and stepped into the bathroom, closing the door behind her. Vaughn sat down on the couch and pushed up the sleeves of his black sweater. He thought about turning on the TV but resisted. It was Marianna's room, and she was the one who had been attacked. He would wait to see what she wanted to do. He heard the hair dryer hum to life and sat back to wait

When Marianna emerged a few moments later, her hair was up in a high ponytail and her face was makeup-free. She wore cozy slouch socks and a pair of black leggings topped by a huge Harvard sweatshirt. She looked like any other college coed, except she was a touch more beautiful than the average Jane.

"Stylish, huh?" she said, noticing him eyeing her outfit.

"Better," Vaughn replied truthfully.

"Not into glamour girls, then?" Marianna asked, flopping onto the couch beside him. "Actually, I'm not surprised."

"Women don't need all that stuff," Vaughn told her, slumping down a bit, getting comfortable. "I don't know what makes them think they do."

"'Society,'" Marianna joked, making air quotes with her fingers. Then her face fell and she scooted down into the couch as well. "I guess if I hadn't dressed the way I did tonight, Carlos and Roberto would have never—"

"Don't finish that sentence," Vaughn said, his eyes flashing. "You're a smart woman. You know as well as I do that there's no excuse for what those guys did."

Marianna nodded slowly, staring across the room at the blank TV screen. "I still can't believe it. I've known those guys since I was still crawling. We used to finger-paint together, go riding at their father's estate. . . . I guess you never know who you can trust."

Vaughn's thoughts instantly turned to his former

friend, Don Hewitt, a guy he'd trained with at the Farm and grown to trust with his life—until he'd revealed himself to be a traitor and killed Vaughn's mentor, Steve Rice. After that, Vaughn had been certain he'd never trust anyone again. But over the last few months, he'd learned that without trust he and Chloe would never be able to pull off a mission. Sometimes you just had to put your life in someone else's hands. Sometimes there was no other option.

"I hate to ask this, but you don't think they're part of La Rappresaglia, do you?" Vaughn asked.

Marianna scoffed, toying with the hem of her sweatshirt. "They have neither the originality nor the intelligence. That's probably why I always thought they were harmless."

The sorrow in her voice touched Vaughn, but he could think of nothing comforting or wise to say, so he sat there in silence, waiting for Marianna to continue. She was so different now that she'd let her guard down—or had it torn down. Ever since the cops had shown up to haul Carlos and Roberto off, there hadn't been one quip, one insult, one fake flirtation. Vaughn would have almost liked this new Marianna if not for the unfortunate circumstances that had brought her out.

"Do you think La Rappresaglia is going to succeed?" Marianna asked suddenly. Her skin seemed somehow paler in the dim light from the couch-side lamp. "Do you think they'll kill my father?"

"Not if we can do anything about it," Vaughn answered automatically, the words coming out as if they'd been programmed. He knew the CIA would do everything it could, but so far La Rappresaglia wasn't giving them much to go on.

"I'm worried about him. These people seem serious," Marianna said. "My parents try to shelter me from these things, but I'm not stupid. I know what goes on in my own country. I know that the hatred these people feel for my father is real."

She sat up straight as she spoke and tucked one leg under her, turning to face Vaughn. He followed her lead and pushed himself up as well. Serious conversations demanded a more serious posture. He looked into Marianna's eyes and saw something very familiar reflected in their depths.

"You really love your father, don't you?" he asked, hoping he wasn't overstepping his bounds.

"My family is very important to me," Marianna replied firmly. "There's nothing I wouldn't do to protect the people who care for me."

Vaughn felt another tug at his heart, and he glanced down at the flowered pattern on the couch cushion between him and Marianna. Just like Vaughn's father, Toscana had chosen a profession that put him in a dangerous position. The fact that he was an important person who did great things didn't make the constant worry any easier for his family.

"Things are not perfect in Italy right now," Marianna said. "I understand the issues these people have. . . . I do. But I do not believe my father has to die. What will more death solve?"

"Nothing," Vaughn said. "But try getting the rest of the world to believe that."

Marianna smiled and looked down at her hands. "I want to say something I never say," she told him. "I'm sorry for the way I have been acting with you."

A million sarcastic replies flew into Vaughn's head, but he refrained from saying anything. He could tell Marianna was serious, and he didn't want to kill the moment.

She looked up at him tentatively. "I still think I'm too old for a baby-sitter. My parents think of me as a helpless fourteen-year-old. They're always telling me what to do and where to go. . . ."

Here it comes. The "poor little rich girl" speech, Vaughn thought.

"I know what you're thinking, but I'm not spoiled," Marianna said, noting the expression of disapproval on Vaughn's face. "When we are in

Italy, I accept protection when I have functions to attend and responsibilities to fulfill—my father's position puts us all in the spotlight, and it's fine. But this was supposed to be a vacation for me. A vacation from everything. I didn't want some stranger following me around."

Vaughn processed her argument and realized that she did have a point. Yes, there were people in the world who had much bigger problems, but that didn't make Marianna's feelings any less valid. Everyone had issues, no matter what their station in life.

"I understand," Vaughn said finally.

Marianna smiled her thanks.

"But you can't blame them for wanting to take care of you," Vaughn added. "You *are* their only child."

Vaughn saw something flit across Marianna's face at that moment—anger, resentment—something dark. But it was gone so fast, it was easy to believe he had imagined it. Perhaps she hated that all the focus was on her, being the president's only child.

"Well, I *am* glad you were there tonight," she told him, looking away again. "Thank you for that."

"Don't thank me," Vaughn said sincerely. "I only wish I had gotten there sooner."

Marianna smiled, and for the second time that night, they locked eyes. Vaughn felt his heart respond with a thump to her unabashed stare. He found himself dropping his gaze to her perfect, full lips—imagining what she might do if he just leaned forward and—

No! A little voice in his mind called out. He blinked, breaking eye contact, and stood up. *Don't go there,* he thought, wiping his palms against his thighs. *You cannot go there.*

"I'm starving. You want anything from room service?" he asked, crossing to the phone.

"No thanks," Marianna said. She reached for the remote and clicked on the TV. Vaughn felt his shoulders relax as a laugh track blared through the speakers. Just like that, the moment was over, the tension gone.

Just don't let it happen again, he told himself as he dialed room service. *Romance on the job is never a good idea. Especially when you have to answer to Betty Harlow.*

6

THE FOLLOWING MORNING VAUGHN woke up feeling rested, refreshed, and, happily, very unromantic. He dressed quickly in a no-nonsense blue suit with a light blue shirt and dark blue tie. As he buttoned his jacket, he stared at his reflection in the full-length mirror.

"Last night was a blip," he told himself, yanking down his sleeves. "It was the whole damsel-in-distress thing. Nothing more." He took a deep breath, smoothed the front of his jacket, and glared at himself, erasing all thoughts of Marianna and her Botticelli beauty. "Get it together, Vaughn."

Luckily, Marianna was going to be with her mother and father all morning at the UN, and there was enough security there to protect all of Italy, let alone the first family. After that, they had family events planned for the rest of the afternoon. Vaughn had the day off from baby-sitting to help Chloe and review all the evidence she had gathered while he'd been out with Marianna the day before.

No Marianna duty meant no potential flirting situations. Out of sight, out of mind.

Vaughn's cell phone trilled, and he grabbed it from the bedside table where it rested on top of his English-Italian dictionary. He'd decided to spend some time brushing up on his vocabulary the night before just in case he overheard something important. Being with Marianna and her friends at the club had made it abundantly clear that he wasn't quite the Italian expert he'd believed himself to be. He was close, but thanks to ever-changing slang, he was not there yet.

He hit the Answer button and brought the phone to his ear. "Vaughn."

"Hey, it's Chloe. You better get up here. I think you're right about Dominic."

Vaughn's heart slammed into his rib cage. "I'll be right there."

He slipped his cell phone into his pocket,

holstered his gun, and rushed out of the room. One glance down the hallway at the crowd of people waiting for the elevator and he opted for the stairs. He took them two at a time to the HQ floor a couple of stories above, his imagination running away with him. In his mind's eye he saw Dominic holding Marianna hostage; saw him with a gun to the president's head; saw him in dark, clandestine meetings with the other members of La Rappresaglia.

Vaughn felt a hot sheen of perspiration form over his skin as he emerged from the stairwell. What had Chloe discovered? Was Marianna in immediate danger?

The security at the hotel wasn't quite as state-of-the-art as the precautions that secured the Outer Rim. Two agents were stationed on either side of the door to the HQ suite, and even though Vaughn had known them for months, they still checked his ID. As soon as they nodded their approval, he burst into the suite. Chloe, Elena, and Barry all looked up from their computer screens. The thick curtains were drawn to block the glare of the early-morning sun from the monitors, giving the room an ominous, almost funereal feel. Vaughn took a deep breath.

"What did you find?" he asked, quickly crossing the dusky room.

"Elena's tap picked up a conversation early this morning," Chloe told him, rising from her chair. She was uncharacteristically rumpled, and her wide eyes were droopy and rimmed in red, as if she hadn't slept all night. Her hair was braided loosely down her back, and her white shirt was untucked from her slacks, which had deep creases in the fabric.

Vaughn glanced at Elena and Barry. They both looked tired and harried as well. There was a half-empty bottle of Jack Daniel's next to Elena's computer.

"Long night?" Vaughn asked, eyeing the bottle.

"Oh, we'll get to that later," Elena said dismissively.

"Why didn't you call me earlier? I would've been here," Vaughn told Chloe.

"You had a long day yesterday. We called you when we were sure we had something."

"Ignore your sympathies next time," Vaughn told her. "I'm here to do a job."

"Got it," Chloe said with a smile.

Vaughn smiled back. "Good. Now, I assume you have a recording of this conversation." He stood behind Elena and Barry, who were both clicking away at their keyboards. He crossed his arms over his chest, all business.

"Cuing tape . . . now," Barry said. He reached over and flipped a switch on the nearest speaker.

"Pronto?" Dominic's gruff voice boomed from the speakers.

"Sorry!" Barry exclaimed, scrambling to turn down the volume.

"It's me," a male voice replied, much lower than Dominic's. An American male's voice. Barry sat back again. "We got the items you requested. And you might wanna bring a little extra cash. My supplier went above and beyond the call of duty."

"What else did he get?" Dominic asked in English.

"I'd rather not say over the phone, but I *will* say that you won't have any trouble threading the needle with this stuff."

Vaughn and Chloe exchanged a glance, and he actually felt the air sizzle between them. Oh, how Vaughn loved it when a suspect thought he was being clever but instead gave up the whole game. Up to that point the two men could have been talking about anything from drugs to diamonds. But *threading the needle* was a euphemism for aiming at a difficult target. That meant weapons.

There was a short pause on the recording, as if Dominic had also realized his contact's blunder.

Then the bodyguard spoke again. "Where's the meet?"

"There's an old abandoned pizzeria at the corner of Union and Bond in Carroll Gardens, Brooklyn. We'll be there at nine A.M. and we're leaving at five after, so be on time."

Vaughn checked his watch. It was seven-thirty.

"I will be there," Dominic said. Then the line went dead.

"Elena, you are a genius," Vaughn said, walking around the table so he could see her. His fingertips started to tingle the way they always did when he knew he was about to make a collar—as if he already had the suspect in his grasp. He couldn't wait to see the look on that smug Dominic's face when he brought him down.

"I know," Elena replied, shrugging nonchalantly but cracking a smile.

"Well, I wouldn't say *genius,*" Barry protested, leaning back in his seat. "I mean, anyone could have designed that tap."

"Then why didn't *you*?" Elena shot back.

"Hey, I've invented plenty of things you never even would've—"

"Guys!" Chloe shouted, cutting them short. "Can we focus here?"

Elena and Barry shot each other scowls like a couple of feuding kindergartners, but they did as they were told and shut up.

Chloe turned to Vaughn. "One of us got a good night's sleep. One of us wouldn't be able to run a mile without collapsing."

"So I guess I'm going in," Vaughn said, feeling slightly guilty leaving his partner manning the desk. But sometimes it just worked out that way.

"I discussed it with Betty this morning, and yes, that's the plan," Chloe told him, shoving a pencil she was fiddling with through the top of her braid. She leaned over her computer and clicked a few windows closed with her mouse. "You'll go, find a secure spot out of sight, and snap some photos. We have to get Dominic on film accepting the weapons. Any exchange of money would be good to catch as well."

"And, of course, the sellers' faces would be nice," Elena said.

"We'll have a backup team within two blocks," Chloe continued. "Once you get the transaction on film, call backup and they'll take care of Dominic and his contacts."

Vaughn nodded. "I'm going to need to blend in."

"Way ahead of you," Barry blurted out, jumping up from his chair excitedly.

"You're gonna love this," Chloe said under her breath.

Barry walked over to the closet and pulled out what basically looked like a large wad of rags on a hanger. He held it up and away from him as he carried it over to Vaughn.

"I'm going as a hobbit?" Vaughn asked, eyeing the brown, green, and gray clothing.

"A homeless man," Barry corrected him. "It's a rundown neighborhood—an abandoned building. They probably won't even notice you, and if they do, they'll just think you're a squatter."

Vaughn forced a smile as he carefully took the hanger from Barry. It weighed a ton. "Why so heavy?"

"These guys wear lots of layers," Barry said matter-of-factly. "It's a warmth thing. I took a bunch of pictures when I was out patrolling with my brother yesterday, you know, for authenticity—just in case you needed to go undercover. And guess what? You do!"

"Yeah, you definitely outdid me this time, Barry," Elena said with a smirk. "You designed a high-tech pile of dirty laundry."

Barry narrowed his eyes. "Thanks, Barry," Vaughn said. He started to fold the clothing, if it could be called that, over his arm and caught a whiff of the most vile stench he'd ever encountered.

"What is *that*?" he asked, scrunching up his face and trying not to dry heave. It was a good thing he hadn't eaten yet today.

"You've been living on the streets," Barry told him. "It has to be authentic."

"Does it have to be *that* authentic?" Vaughn asked. The stench hit the back of his throat and actually caused his vision to temporarily blur. "Couldn't I be a homeless man who just visited a shelter and got cleaned up?"

Barry's face fell. "Hadn't thought of that."

"You'll get used to it," Chloe said, slapping Vaughn on the back. She moved away quickly, however, when she realized she was within sniffing range. "Elena, why don't you show Vaughn what you have for him?" she suggested as she stepped to the opposite end of the table, holding her breath.

Elena reached for the Jack Daniel's bottle and handed it to Vaughn. He tipped it to the side and looked it over skeptically.

"Okay, I know you guys want me to be authentic, but I don't think I should be drunk for this job," he joked.

"It's a camera," Elena told him. "It's not alcohol, just colored water."

Vaughn unscrewed the cap and swigged. Yep, just water. But upon further inspection, he couldn't find anything cameralike about the bottle—no lens, no buttons, nothing.

"I give up," he said, handing the bottle back to her.

Elena tightened the cap and held the bottle up sideways with the black-and-white label facing Vaughn.

"Keep an eye on Jack's face," she instructed him.

When Elena unscrewed the cap again, Jack Daniel's face slid away, revealing a tiny lens beneath. Vaughn blinked and leaned in toward the lens, impressed. He never would have noticed it if Elena hadn't pointed it out to him.

"That's amazing," he said.

"It gets better," Chloe told him.

"Don't move," Elena said. Then she blew a breath into the bottle and Vaughn heard the tiniest, softest of clicks. Instantly his face, up close and personal, with one nostril the size of a small planet, appeared on Elena's computer screen.

"What the—"

Elena tilted the bottle toward Vaughn. "See that tiny chip on the inside of the bottle?" she asked.

Vaughn peeked through the back of the bottle,

and sure enough, there was a flat computer chip on the glass, hidden by the label on the front.

"It's heat sensitive. You breathe into the bottle, and as long as you're not dead, it'll trigger the camera."

"If he were dead, he wouldn't be breathing," Barry pointed out.

Elena rolled her eyes. "I just meant he'd have to be above room temperature to—"

"Aren't we always?" Barry challenged her. "I mean, unless we *are* dead, in which case we're not breathing."

"Exactly my point!" Elena argued. "Why do you have to—"

"Okay! Okay! We're splitting hairs here, people," Chloe said, throwing her hands up and stepping between the two techies. "We need to get Vaughn ready."

"We also have a regular video camera for you in case you get yourself in a position to use it," Elena said, holding out a silver digital camera the size of her palm.

"Thanks," Vaughn said, plucking it out of her hand. "This I know how to use."

"Okay, let's get to work," Chloe said, returning to her computer. "We have a lot to do."

"Time to get dressed?" Barry asked, raising

his eyebrows and nodding toward his odiferous creation.

Vaughn grimaced. "Let's save that for last."

*   *   *

Vaughn sat on the steps of the crumbling building next door to the pizzeria where Dominic and his contact were set to meet. The sun beat down on him from above, and he started to wish that Barry hadn't gone for quite so many layers. Breathing through his mouth to avoid his own stench, he leaned back on his elbows, going for a lazy pose and stretching out to keep cool. All the while he kept watch on the next building. Waiting.

A white van pulled up at the corner, and two men dressed in brown coveralls emerged from the front. Wearing baseball caps pulled low, they walked around to the back of the van and opened the doors. A third figure stepped out, but this one was obviously a woman. Her hair was stuffed up under her cap, and she was wearing glasses. Together, the three started to unload wooden crates onto the sidewalk.

"We have two men and one woman unloading a white Dodge van, license plate number Charlie Harriet Charlie two two five," Vaughn said into his remote mike. Anything he said would be picked up by the backup team and by Chloe and the others back at HQ. He could hear both Chloe and Agent Green, the leader of the backup team, in his tiny earpiece.

"Roger that," Chloe said.

Vaughn lifted his bottle to his lips and breathed into it a few times, snapping photos of the men and the woman, of the van, of its license plate. He didn't recognize any of the suspects from his distance, but Chloe and Elena might be able to enhance the photographs and find them on the CIA's database.

The suspects brought the crates into the pizza place through a side door, making several trips until the van was empty. Then the woman came out again and closed up the vehicle. She was turned partially away from him, but Vaughn saw her lift her wrist to her mouth and speak into it. A remote microphone.

"Female suspect wired with audio. Not sure about the other two," Vaughn said.

"Okay. Give it ten minutes, then move in," Chloe responded.

Vaughn checked the clock tower across the street as the woman made her way back inside. He was to wait the ten minutes in order to give the suspects time to make sure the place was clear. Then he'd sneak in through the basement door he'd checked out earlier. It was unlocked, and thanks to a small bottle of oil Barry had supplied him with, it was now also not squeaky.

Vaughn waited impatiently as the minute hand on the clock inched forward. At 8:54 he pushed himself up from the stairs, then loped around to the back of the brick-walled pizzeria and ducked along the wall under boarded-up windows.

The basement was dark, musty, and cold. Metal shelves along the walls held dust-covered vats marked TOMATO SAUCE and FLOUR. It took Vaughn's eyes a moment to adjust as he made his way over to the bottom of the stairs, where a mouse skittered across his path.

"I'm in," Vaughn whispered. "Going radio silent now." He reached up and pushed a flat button on the tiny mechanism beneath his bottom layer of clothing—a legitimately ancient CBGB T-shirt. Where Barry had found it, Vaughn had no idea. He heard the hum of the signal go dead in his ear, effectively shutting out Chloe and Green. If he got close enough to the action, their transmissions might give him away.

Vaughn looked up toward the open doorway at the top of the stairs. He saw no movement and still heard no voices.

So far so good, he thought. He placed his foot on the bottom step, which let out a loud creak.

Vaughn instantly drew his foot away and waited, his heart pounding.

Nice one, he told himself, shaking his head. He tried again, this time keeping close to the wall, where the stairs were reinforced and sure to be at their sturdiest. Moving slowly, he made it all the way up the steps without another scare.

Checking around the corner, Vaughn saw that he was now in the kitchen. Most of the major appliances had been torn free from the walls and carted off, leaving dangling electric, gas, and water lines protruding from ragged holes in the tile. A window was cut out of the far wall, built there so that the chef could pass dishes through to the servers in the dining room. Vaughn saw a shadow move on the other side of the window and jumped back for a moment. He pulled out the tiny video camera Elena had given him and set it to record. If he could get the thing positioned on that window ledge, he could tape everything that went down in the next room.

A quick rap sounded on the front door, and Vaughn heard rustling and footsteps moving away from him. This was his chance. He slipped out of the doorway and over to the serving window. The three suspects all had their backs to him as they answered the door. Vaughn positioned the camera near the corner of the ledge, trained on the crates piled in the center of the dining room. He quickly ducked down again, pressed his back against the wall, and pulled out a small monitor. He flipped it on and smiled. There, framed perfectly in the shot, were Dominic and the three suspects from the van. Whatever happened in that room, he was going to get it all.

Vaughn glanced across the kitchen toward the back door to his left. Ideally he should get the hell out of there now and let the camera do its job. He didn't need the device—it was transmitting a signal directly to Elena's computer back at the hotel. But moving now was too risky. If the dealers heard any noise, they'd be on him in less than a second, and even with Barry's disguise, Dominic would obviously recognize him. He was going to have to keep quiet and wait it out.

"You brought the cash?" one of the men asked.

On his tiny screen, Vaughn saw a woman enter the room carrying a briefcase, which she handed to Dominic. He placed the briefcase on one of the few tables that was not toppled over or broken, popped open the latches, and lifted the top. Vaughn had to restrain himself to keep from whistling. There had to be a couple of million dollars inside.

That Cartier heist did La Rappresaglia well, he thought, gripping the tiny monitor.

The men inspected the contents of the briefcase while the woman held back, hovering near the crates. She kept her back to the camera, almost as if she sensed it was there.

"Let us see what you brought," Dominic said.

One of the men walked over to the first crate. He picked up a crowbar from the lid and started to pry it open, while the other man went to work on the crate nearest Vaughn. The first man quickly popped the top of his crate free and tossed it aside, revealing two sleek air rifles, each fitted with distance-targeting systems. The guns had been packed carefully in shredded paper. The seller stood up, smiling in Dominic's direction.

It was almost over. All they had to do was make the exchange. Then Vaughn would break radio silence, call in Green and his team, and victory would be theirs.

Then, right before Vaughn's eyes, the woman whipped a gun out of her coveralls and shot the first man right in the chest. Vaughn's heart hit his throat as the man's eyes widened in surprise. He clutched his chest and fell forward, toppling over the open crate. Vaughn realized at once that it wasn't a bullet that had hit the man, but a tranquilizer dart. Still, all hell broke loose in the next room. The second man went at the woman with his crowbar as Dominic stood there, momentarily stunned. The woman easily fought the second man off, knocking him unconscious with the heavy lid from one of the crates. She had perfect moves—professional moves— moves Vaughn had learned in his first weeks at the Farm.

"Don't even think it," the woman said, pulling a pistol from an ankle holster. Her back was still to the camera as she trained her weapon on Dominic, who was now headed for the kitchen—for Vaughn's hiding place. Vaughn clenched his teeth, watching Dominic on the screen even though he was no more than two feet away, just beyond the door that led to the dining room. Dominic clutched the briefcase to his chest as he stared at the gun.

"Who do you work for?" the woman demanded.

"*L'Italia,*" Dominic answered. "I work for my president. President Ramero Toscana."

"I know who you *supposedly* work for," the woman said, her tone intimidating. "But who do you represent here today? La Rappresaglia?"

Vaughn's mind reeled. What the hell was going on here? Who was this woman, and who did *she* work for? The FBI? The NSA? Why hadn't his team been informed that someone else was on this case?

"No!" Dominic protested. "La Rappresaglia is an enemy of the state. I don't—"

"Enough!" the woman barked.

In a flash, she crossed to Dominic and whacked the briefcase out of his arms. It came flying into the kitchen and hit the wall across from Vaughn, popping open and spilling cash everywhere. Dominic threw a punch at the woman, but she ducked, grabbed his arm, and twisted it behind him. As she slammed him up against the wall Vaughn was leaning against, the whole partition shook. Dust spilled down from above, settling over Vaughn and his monitor. Vaughn felt a scratching in his throat, a tightness in his chest as he breathed in the debris. His eyes watered. He tried to hold back, but it was no use. He was done for.

Coughing harshly, Vaughn ran and grabbed the video camera.

The woman's cap had fallen off in the scuffle, and silky brown hair now tumbled out. In a split second Vaughn took in her full lips, her high cheekbones, her bewildered eyes behind her glasses. She was young. His eyes traveled to the floor and he saw that the second man she'd subdued was Mr. Blond. They were the couple from the bar at Trick.

"Who are you?" the young woman demanded, never loosening her grip on Dominic.

Vaughn blinked. Then he ran.

He slammed through the back door to the pizzeria, shedding his long, heavy overcoat and yanking his sweater off over his head. Leaving a trail of clothing behind him, Vaughn ran as fast as he could, but he could feel the woman bearing down on him. His many layers slowed him down, but thanks to Barry, he had a plan for just such a situation.

Vaughn made a left on the next block, scurried up a set of steps, and burst into the gym attached to St. Agatha's Roman Catholic Church, which had long ago been converted into a homeless shelter. Just as Barry had promised, the place was packed with people dressed exactly like Vaughn. He dove into the crowd around the kitchen, where breakfast was being served, raced past the volunteers at the ovens and stoves, and went out another door to Hoyt Street, where his getaway car was parked.

Vaughn peeled out and pressed the button on his mike. "Move in! Move in! Two suspects down, two more at large. The woman may be in or around St. Agatha's on Hoyt Street." He took a deep breath, hating what he was about to admit. "Dominic Rizzio's whereabouts unknown."

"Copy that. We're going in," Green replied.

Vaughn pulled back and slammed the heel of his hand into his steering wheel. He ripped the microphone and earpiece off and tossed them on the floor, then popped open the glove compartment to fish out his cell phone to call Chloe.

What the hell had just happened?

And why was his heart suddenly flip-flopping like crazy?

To: reginald.wilson@credit-dauphine.com
From: sydney.bristow@credit-dauphine.com
Subject: La Rappresaglia

To confirm my phone message, mission failed. "Homeless man" interfered with operation—suspect in possession of high-tech video surveillance camera. True identity unknown.

Full report to come. I hope there's some intel SD-6 can salvage.

I'm on my way home. I'll see you at 8 A.M. I'm sorry.

Sydney

7

A CAB HEADING STRAIGHT for Vaughn missed his left headlight by centimeters. Horns honked, drivers cursed out their windows at him, and a little old lady actually gave him the finger, but Vaughn couldn't have cared less. All he could think about was Marianna. When he'd reached Chloe by phone, she had said that she and Marianna were on their way back to the hotel after an outing with the first lady.

If Dominic had gotten away, he had a head start. Plus a couple of crates full of state-of-the-art weaponry.

That was why Vaughn found himself navigating

his car along the median that separated north- and southbound traffic on the East Side Highway.

Cutting the wheel, Vaughn sliced through a yellow light, taking the 23rd Street exit into the heart of the city. Pressing down on the gas and willing pedestrians to stay on the sidewalk, he spun onto Third Avenue and kept his eyes on the traffic lights ahead. Midmorning traffic wasn't half as bad as lunchtime or rush hour, and Vaughn counted himself lucky as he watched the street signs fly by, their numbers getting higher and higher.

He had to get back to the hotel before Dominic did. But he also recognized the possibility that if Dominic was part of the conspiracy, other members of the president's security detail might be as well.

Vaughn skidded to a stop in front of the hotel and jumped out of the car. As he raced past the uniformed doorman, the guy called after him to move his vehicle, but Vaughn ignored him. The hotel was crawling with federal officers and NYPD, thanks to the event at the UN. Someone would recognize the auto as government property and deal with the angry cabbies and hotel staff.

Sprinting across the lobby, Vaughn shouted to a group of well-dressed senior citizens to hold the elevator. They appeared startled when they saw him coming, and Vaughn couldn't figure out why until he saw his reflection in the gold doors of the elevator. He still looked—and smelled—like a street rat.

"Federal agent!" Vaughn shouted to them, whipping out his badge for all to see. "I need this elevator."

The seniors stepped back to let him in, and Vaughn smiled his thanks. His face fell when he saw a couple of the elderly women holding their noses and turning their faces away. He was going to have to remember to drop-kick Barry later.

The doors slid closed, and Vaughn used his special code to send the elevator zipping up to Marianna's secure floor. Vaughn practiced keeping his cool, regulating his breathing and keeping his feet from tapping. Everything was going to be fine. Chloe was probably sitting with Marianna in her room right now, chatting about clothes or makeup or whatever it was women chatted about.

The elevator beeped, announcing its arrival, and Vaughn stepped out into the hallway, making a quick right to head for Marianna's room. The two guards stationed outside her door stepped aside instantly when they saw him coming. No doubt Chloe had told them he was on his way.

Vaughn took a deep breath and entered Marianna's room. As he'd predicted, she and Chloe were sitting on the couch in front of the TV, talking. Contrary to what he'd predicted, they had a NASCAR race roaring on the television screen and were lamenting the shoddy work of one of the pit crews.

A big sigh of relief escaped Vaughn's lips, but it was short-lived. The second Marianna turned and caught his eye, he recalled the news he had to deliver. He didn't relish her reaction when he informed her that her most trusted bodyguard couldn't, in fact, be trusted.

"Agent Vaughn!" Chloe said, rising from the couch. She was looking much more herself now in a sleek gray suit and white shirt, her hair drawn up in a modern bun. "I see you didn't have time to change your clothes," she said, wrinkling her nose.

"I came right up," Vaughn replied, glancing at Marianna.

"Is everything okay?" Marianna asked, draping her arm over the back of the flowered couch. She pursed her lips and gave him a slight, teasing smile. "You look like death."

"Smell like it too," Chloe said, scrunching her nose as she approached her partner.

"Thanks a lot," Vaughn said with a short laugh.

"So . . . I'll leave you guys to it, then," Chloe said. She shot Vaughn an encouraging look before exiting the room. The door clicked shut softly behind her, and Marianna reached for the remote and muted the television, plunging the suite into perfect silence. Even the regular city noises from the street below were blocked out at this altitude.

"Leave us to what?" Marianna asked, standing to face him. She was wearing a cream-colored slip dress and pearls, and he heard the soft swish of her pantyhose as her legs moved. "Michael, what is going on? We were about to have tea, but Agent Murphy said there had been a change of plans and escorted me to my room without telling me why. I thought—" She paused. "I thought something might have happened to you," she finished, looking into his eyes in a way that made his whole body clench.

"I'm fine. Nothing happened to me," Vaughn said.

Marianna's features relaxed slightly and she sank back down into the couch.

Vaughn sat down too.

"What is it, then?" Marianna asked. "What happened?"

"There's no easy way to tell you this," Vaughn began, pressing his hands into his thighs. "We think . . . in fact, we're fairly certain that Dominic is involved with the effort to assassinate your father. He's a member of La Rappresaglia."

Marianna began to laugh. "Dominic? It's not possible," she said, wiping at the corner of her eye with her fingertips. "Dominic has been my body-guard for years. He would never betray my family."

"I'm sorry, Marianna, but he has," Vaughn told her, swallowing hard. "I saw him buying weapons. I saw it with my own eyes."

"No, Vaughn, *I'm* sorry," Marianna replied, quickly growing serious. "Dominic's family has been in the service of the Italian government for generations. They take their commitment very seriously. If Dominic was buying weapons, it was only to use them to protect us, not to hurt us."

Vaughn took a deep breath. He had to admire Marianna's loyalty to her constant companion. He only wished Dominic had the same loyalty to her. There was no doubt in his mind that Dominic was dangerous, but how could he convince Marianna of that if she was going to be so stubborn?

Then it hit him. The videotape. It was against policy. But it was the only way.

"There's something you need to see," Vaughn said quietly.

Marianna opened her mouth to speak, but she never had the chance to say a word. Suddenly Vaughn and Marianna were grabbed roughly from behind, soaked handkerchiefs secured over their mouths. There was the sweet scent of liquid chloroform . . . the struggle to resist . . .

And then he blacked out.

8

THE PAIN WAS LIKE nothing Vaughn had ever felt before. His brain seemed to be trying to expand, pressing against his skull, pounding and tightening, pounding and tightening. He opened his eyes and the light assaulted them, sending a new shock wave of pain straight through his cranium. He pressed his eyes closed again, hot tears stinging at their corners, and tried to use his hands for an added shield, but he couldn't move them. His arms were tied behind his back, secured to a solid metal chair. When he tried to move his legs, he found that his ankles were bound as well. Fighting off a sudden bout of nausea, Vaughn breathed in slowly through his nose and out through his mouth.

This is not good. Very, very not good, Vaughn thought groggily. He shook his head slowly, ignoring the pain, and tried to focus. He had to figure out where he was—and whether Marianna was still with him. Vaughn took a deep breath and concentrated. Using his eyes, for the moment, was not an option. What could he smell? What could he feel? What could he hear?

There were voices, low and urgent, somewhere off to his right and in front of him. The sound echoed slightly, leading Vaughn to believe he was in a large room, maybe a warehouse. The air was bitingly cold, as it would be in an open, unheated space. Vaughn was still in the thin CBGB T-shirt and his bare arms were covered with goose bumps. Beyond the scent of chloroform that still clung to his nostrils, Vaughn could smell stale dust and dirt. If it was a warehouse, it probably hadn't been used for a long time. Beyond the voices were the sounds of rushing traffic, the occasional screeching of brakes. Wherever he was, he was very close to a major roadway. That, at least, was a plus when it came to escape.

Behind his eyelids, Vaughn's eyes were gradually adjusting to the onslaught of light. He blinked them open again and ignored the tears that formed.

The room yawned in front of him like a huge cave. Row upon row of tiny windows near the two-story-high ceiling let in streams of bright white light from outside. The walls appeared to be made of cheap, corrugated steel that had rusted and rotted out in places along the cement floor. To his left and right were shelves packed with crates, boxes, and sacks, some new, some covered in decades' worth of dust. Vaughn inspected the shelves quickly but didn't see any crates that resembled the ones Dominic had attempted to purchase.

Across the room, in the more open end of the building, two black vans were parked—no license plates, no markings. Directly behind the vans was a large, wooden double door that could be opened for vehicles to drive through. Another door stood to Vaughn's left, secured by a sturdy-looking padlock. Vaughn knew that if he was going to escape, those double doors clear across the football field–sized warehouse were his only hope.

Somewhere behind the second van the kidnappers were powwowing. Vaughn could hear unintelligible voices and the scrape of feet against the silt-covered ground. There was no sign of Marianna. Vaughn felt a chill run through him. If he had failed in his duty . . . if anything had happened to her . . . he would never forgive himself.

Okay, think. They used chloroform, so I've probably been out for about an hour, Vaughn rationalized. *Chloe definitely knows I'm gone, and I had my cell phone on me, so she might be able to use the tracking device to pinpoint my location.*

Of course, that could take half a day. And who knew what these people would do to him and to Marianna in the meantime? What they might have already done . . .

A sudden groan very close to Vaughn's right ear caused him to flinch. He strained his neck to look over his shoulder, and relief instantly flooded his body. Marianna sat a couple of feet behind him, just out of his natural line of vision. Like Vaughn, she was also tied to a chair, and her head lolled around on her neck as she began to awaken. She was alive.

"Marianna, it's me," Vaughn whispered. "Don't open your eyes."

"Michael? Why not?" Marianna whispered back. Then she opened her eyes and groaned, pulling her head back.

"Because it really hurts," Vaughn replied quietly, now stating the obvious.

"Where are we?" Marianna mumbled.

"Somewhere in the city, I think," Vaughn told her. "I'm guessing downtown. There are still a lot of abandoned warehouses in the meatpacking district."

Suddenly, the voices in the far corner grew louder and the sounds of movement increased. The kidnappers had heard them talking. Vaughn's senses went on high alert, and he steeled himself for whatever was to come.

Four men emerged from around the side of the van, each of them dressed in army fatigues, their faces covered by green ski masks. Only their eyes were visible. They wore black leather gloves, and two of them—the two in the center—carried automatic pistols. Vaughn was outnumbered and outarmed, but still he felt a surge of hope. It could have been worse. There could have been more men. They could have *all* been toting guns. The guns could have been Uzis. Perhaps La Rappresaglia wasn't such a formidable foe after all.

"Gli ospiti svegliano," one of the guards in the center of the line said, his voice booming. *"Dite buon giorno!"*

Vaughn's arms tensed as the two unarmed guards walked up to him and Marianna. The man before him raised his left arm to strike, and Vaughn's first instinct was to turn his head to the right to lessen the impact, but he wouldn't give them the satisfaction. He braced himself as the man's beefy arm swung down and backhanded him across the cheek. His eye felt as if it were going to explode as his face snapped to the side. Marianna cried out next to him, and Vaughn clenched his teeth, staring down the man who had given the order.

"I thought the Italians were a welcoming people," he spat. "That's how you say good morning?"

"Agent Vaughn, is it?" the man addressed him in English, his Italian accent thick, making his words clipped. "You arrogant Americans believe you can do a better job of protecting Miss Toscana than her own men. See the fruits of your success?"

He laughed, spreading his arms wide, and the others around him chuckled. Vaughn narrowed his eyes, tucking what had been said into the back of his mind. Those comments sounded like they came from someone who was personally offended by his existence—someone who *was* one of Marianna's own men and resented his presence. Carefully Vaughn checked out his captors—what he could see of them—and saw that Dominic was not among them. None of them had Dominic's lazy brown eyes or his massive square shoulders. If Dominic was involved, he had made the wise decision to stay away from this particular mission. But these men could be part of the president's security detail.

"What do you want from us?" Vaughn asked. "Is La Rappresaglia in the habit of kidnapping innocent young women? Is that part of your cause?" As he spoke, he twisted his wrists back and forth carefully, the ropes shredding his skin. It was painful, but he could feel the binds begin to loosen, making him want to struggle even more. But he had to be careful and keep his movements imperceptible. They couldn't know he was trying to break free.

"Do not pretend to be so naïve," the man in charge said, waving his gun around in front of him. "The sins of the father are often visited on his children."

He walked over to Marianna, his thick boots clomping on the cement floor, and hovered over her. "We have contacted your father, Miss Toscana. We have made an offer. We give you to him, he surrenders to us."

"My father will never give in to you," Marianna retorted, her voice full of unshed tears.

The man stared at them. "If he does not contact us within the hour, we will kill you."

Vaughn continued to work his hands. He knew enough about these people to realize that they weren't just going to let them sit here for an hour and wait for their deaths. These men were heartless, ruthless, violent. If they were going to use Marianna's execution to send a message, they would want her body to be mutilated when it was found. He had to figure out a way to escape before these men did Marianna any more harm.

"I wish I could stay and chat, but I have a telephone call to wait for," the ringleader continued. He looked at his two unarmed henchmen, and his eyes crinkled at the corners as if he was grinning under his mask. *"Divertitevi!"*

Have fun, Vaughn translated as the leader and his other buddy walked off toward the vans again. He definitely didn't like the sound of that. The two lackeys left behind approached him and Marianna. As Vaughn quickened the movement of his wrists, he felt his skin burning and ripping, but the ropes were growing looser and looser. When the man in front of him pulled a large, jagged blade from his waistband, Vaughn's ropes fell free. He kept his arms in the same position, though, pretending he was still bound.

"Michael!" Marianna moaned. The man in front of her had an identical blade poised along her cheekbone.

Vaughn held his breath. He had one moment to save their lives. One moment to play this right. The guard leaned over him, brandishing his weapon, muttering insults in Italian. The second Vaughn was able to see the gold flecks in the man's eyes, he pulled both arms around, grabbed the surprised man on either side of his head, and snapped his neck.

Marianna's attacker was temporarily frozen in shock as the man crumbled at Vaughn's feet. Vaughn dove forward, grabbed the man's blade, and quickly severed the ropes that bound his legs. As he did, Marianna's attacker lunged at his back with his knife. Vaughn whirled out of the way, swung around with his weapon, and sliced a deep cut in the man's arm. He cried out in pain, and Vaughn knew he had less than a second before the two gun-toting psychos came to the rescue.

He picked up his chair, raised it over the guy's head, and flattened him, then yanked his knife from his limp grip. Just as he grabbed the back of Marianna's chair, the leader and his friend reappeared from behind the vans. Vaughn dragged Marianna's chair behind the shelves next to her as the kidnappers aimed their guns.

Suddenly, the wall behind Vaughn exploded with a series of shots. He got to his knees behind Marianna and sliced her hands free. Then he handed her the extra knife and went to work on her left leg as she went to work on her right.

"We cannot survive this," Marianna said as she jumped to her feet.

Vaughn pushed her to the floor and crouched next to her behind the huge crates on the bottom shelves. Unfortunately, he was inclined to agree. The men had seen where they'd hidden themselves, and any moment they would be hemmed in from both sides.

"Give up, Vaughn!" the leader called, his voice echoing. "We know where you are!"

Vaughn looked around for some kind of weapon. He checked on the shelves, then dropped to the ground to check under them, but he found nothing. Then Marianna tugged on his arm and pointed up. The shelves were fashioned out of a series of horizontal silver bars, forming a kind of ladder. If he and Marianna could climb up there and get through to the other side, they might be able to get to the vans before the two kidnappers realized what had happened.

It wasn't a perfect plan, but it was all they had.

Marianna met his eyes. She could do this.

"Lose the shoes," he whispered, nodding at her high heels.

Marianna stepped out of her expensive shoes without hesitation and grasped the first rung of the shelving. She looked at Vaughn for confirmation, and he nodded.

"Go!" Vaughn whispered as a bullet popped open a bag near his shoulder. Meatpacking salt poured onto the floor at his feet, creating a pebbly mountain.

Marianna started to climb and made it to the fourth shelf. She looked down at him, then slipped onto the huge shelf, disappearing from sight.

Vaughn could hear the kidnappers getting closer. He climbed up after Marianna and found her cowering on the wide ledge. He slipped in after her, and they both kept down as flat as they could get. The two kidnappers were still in sight, one inching around the side of the shelves to the right, the other to the left.

"The second they're out of view, I jump, then you," Vaughn whispered to Marianna.

She nodded her understanding, the kidnappers disappeared from the corners of his vision, and Vaughn threw himself off the shelf. His feet hit hard, and Marianna jumped into his arms. His heart slamming into his rib cage, Vaughn grabbed her hand and took off for the vans, expecting every second to hear gunfire exploding behind him.

"Dove sono?" he heard one of the men ask.

"Get in!" Vaughn called, releasing Marianna's

hand. He jumped behind the wheel of the nearest van, and Marianna climbed in next to him. The second they were seated, the side mirror was taken off by a bullet. The shots came one right after the other, hitting the grill, the roof, the bumper. *Bam! Bam! Bam!*

Thank God for bad aim, Vaughn thought. He reached for the ignition and nearly shouted for joy when he felt a key ring in his grasp. As he started the car, shots pelted the windshield.

"Get down!" Vaughn shouted to Marianna.

Vaughn ducked down next to her, slammed the gearshift into reverse, and hit the gas. The van screeched backward and smashed through the wooden doors behind it, eliciting a scream from Marianna. Vaughn spun the wheel and looked up. The alley was barely visible through all the spiderweb cracks in the windshield. He ducked until he could see through a small corner at the bottom left of the glass, put the car in drive, and took off.

The van flew out onto the highway, cutting off three lanes of traffic and leaving a nasty accident in its wake. Vaughn wove his way in and out among moving cars for the second time that day. This time *he* was being pursued. The second van was on his tail. "Look around for a cell phone or a radio," Vaughn told Marianna. "Anything."

Marianna unlatched the glove compartment

and it fell open, spilling documents, sunglasses, and a half-eaten bag of potato chips into her lap and onto the floor. Marianna sifted through it all and came up with an old, very large cell phone.

"There's this," she said, holding it up.

A bullet hit the back of the van, shattering one of the two windows, and Vaughn cursed under his breath. The light in front of him turned red and he gunned the engine, twisting the wheel to the right. Barely missing a head-on collision, Vaughn cut off a couple of cabs, got off the highway, and sped down Fourteenth Street.

"See if it works," he told Marianna. He was sweating like a fiend but totally focused. For a moment he thought he had lost the second van, but then he saw it swing around the corner a couple of blocks back, still coming on fast.

"It does," Marianna said, holding up the phone.

"Dial 310-555-7272 and tell Agent Murphy we're being pursued eastbound on Fourteenth Street by an unmarked black van. Tell her ours is damaged, theirs isn't. Got it?" He looked up and saw that traffic ahead was blocked. "Damn. I'm turning up Eighth."

Marianna punched in the number and was blurting out the message when Chloe picked up. Vaughn cut the wheel left and started up Eighth Avenue, heading for midtown. The last thing he wanted was to hit tourist central with all its innocent people and pedestrian roadblocks, but he didn't have much of a choice at this point.

He ran a couple of more lights and was clipped by a BMW traveling west. The van was thrown off course momentarily, but Vaughn spun the wheel and got the vehicle under control again. Luckily he seemed to be putting more distance between him and his pursuers.

Then it happened: midtown traffic. Everything was jammed, and Vaughn was forced to hit the brakes.

"What do we do?" Marianna asked desperately.

Vaughn stared in the rearview mirror. The other van was inching ever closer, stopping and starting as it lurched from lane to lane, trying to get to them. Any second Vaughn expected to see the kidnappers jump out of the van and come after them on foot. It would be a stupid move in such a packed neighborhood, but at this point he was thinking that La Rappresaglia's bloodlust heavily outweighed their logic.

"They're gaining on us!" Marianna said with a whimper. "Michael! We need to run!"

Vaughn was about to agree with her. There didn't appear to be any other option. Maybe they could get lost in the never-ending crowds on Broadway.

"Okay," he said. "On the count of three, get out and we'll make a left. Got it?"

"I . . . I don't know if I can—"

And then Vaughn heard the sweetest sound he'd ever heard. Sirens. He glanced in the mirror again and saw two patrol cars descend upon the other van. The cops jumped out and trained their weapons on the vehicle. Seconds later, two more cars hemmed Vaughn's van in, their lights flashing.

Thank you, Chloe, Vaughn thought.

"Raise your hands!" he told Marianna as the officers pointed their guns at the van.

A tear rolled down Marianna's cheek as she put her trembling hands in the air. Vaughn did the same and nodded his reassurance to her.

"Everything's going to be fine now," he said, watching in the mirror as the police officers flattened the kidnappers against the side of their van.

Soon the cops were pulling Vaughn and Marianna out of their vehicle. Chloe was there in seconds, and everything was explained. The moment the police officers stepped away from them, Marianna fell into Michael's arms, sobbing against his chest.

Uncertain as to what the Farm would say was

proper protocol, he put an arm around her as she cried.

"I thought I was going to die," she said into his dirty, smelly shirt. "If you hadn't been there . . ."

She looked up at him, her eyes wide and thankful, and suddenly, protocol was out the window. He felt like a hero. An honest, actual, modern-day hero. He reached up and wiped a tear from her cheek.

"You're safe now," he said, looking into her eyes, his heart pounding. "I'm not going to let anyone hurt you."

9

VAUGHN STOOD IN HIS hotel bathroom, hands braced on either side of the marble sink as he leaned in toward the foggy mirror to check out his bruise. The kidnapper's punch had left a lovely red welt along the side of his eye, but fortunately it didn't look like it was going to darken to purple. If there was one thing Vaughn hated, it was showing up to work looking like he'd had his butt handed to him.

He took a deep breath and let it out slowly, straightening up. It felt good to be clean again, free of Barry's smelly disguise. He slipped into a freshly pressed shirt, savoring the feel of the cool fabric against his skin.

I wonder how Marianna's doing, Vaughn thought, guessing that she too had hit the shower the second she'd returned. Now she was sequestered in the presidential suite with her parents, deciding what to do next.

For his part, Vaughn was due upstairs at the temporary HQ to go over the new information with his CIA colleagues. A team had taken custody of the kidnappers. Chloe was prepping a report on their identities and their records while other agents interrogated them about La Rappresaglia's plans. What Vaughn really wanted to know was whether Dominic had been apprehended.

There was a quick rap on his door, and as Vaughn stepped out of the bathroom, Chloe entered. She had her serious game face on—lips pursed, eyes steady.

"What's up?" Vaughn asked, tucking in his shirt. He reached for the tie draped over a hook on the bathroom door.

"Three of the men they brought in are on the president's payroll, and one is the brother of one of the suspects," Chloe said, tapping her fingers on the top of one of Vaughn's bedside tables. "Toscana confirmed it himself."

"I knew it," Vaughn said, shaking his head. "Marianna and I were taken way too easily. Whoever did it had to have total access to her and her family."

"Yep. And they've already copped to being members of La Rappresaglia."

"That's great," Vaughn said, working on his tie.

"Except for the fact that they say the assassin is still at large and they're refusing to give us any more information," Chloe told him. She pressed her hand against her forehead and sighed. "The president and his family are freaking out. They can't believe so many of the people they trusted are involved in this."

"What about Dominic?" Vaughn asked, yanking on his suit jacket.

"They just brought him in," Chloe said.

Vaughn's heart thumped. Dominic was here? "Why didn't you say so in the first place?" He headed for the door, already planning out his questions and demands. There was something about Dominic that made Vaughn salivate to knock him down a few pegs.

Chloe grabbed his arm, stopping him in his tracks. The strength of her grip momentarily surprised him. It was easy for Vaughn to forget that his fresh-faced colleague had gone through the same training he had—and that she'd excelled at some of the physical tasks it had taken Vaughn a touch longer to master. "Vaughn, are you sure you want to be the one to interrogate him?"

"Why wouldn't I be?" Vaughn asked, his brow knitting.

"I don't know. This just seems kind of . . . personal to you now," she replied, clearly not liking the fact that she had to say it. "The way Marianna was clinging to you in the street earlier—"

"She was just scared," Vaughn said, cutting her off. Much to his chagrin, he felt an embarrassed flush rising up his neck. "I'm not biased, Chloe. I just want to see what this guy has to say for himself." It was a lie, but a tiny white one. Even if he was slightly anti-Dominic, that didn't mean he couldn't do his job.

"Okay," Chloe said with a shrug. "But you should know that while the others have admitted guilt, Dominic's denying any involvement with La Rappresaglia."

"There's a shocker," Vaughn said.

Chloe scolded him for his sarcasm with one scathing look. "Let's go."

The guards outside the door to HQ scanned their IDs as always. Then Vaughn opened the door and let Chloe pass through. Together they approached the suite's bedroom, which had been cleared of its bed and dresser and turned into an interrogation room.

"Agent Vaughn would like to speak to the suspect," Chloe told the guard standing watch.

He nodded, pulled out a key that was attached to his belt by a thick wire, and unlocked the door. Vaughn looked into Chloe's unsure eyes and smiled.

"I'll be fine."

"Take this," Chloe said. She grabbed a file from next to her computer and handed it to him. "It has information on the other detainees. You might be able to use it."

"Thanks." Vaughn entered the room and found Dominic, wrists locked together and chained to his tethered ankles by thick links, sitting at a table in the center of the room. The moment he saw Vaughn, his face hardened and he turned away.

"So, they tell me that you're saying you're innocent," Vaughn began, crossing the room. He tossed the file onto the table and stood across from Dominic, his arms folded over his chest.

"That is right," Dominic said.

"Then what were you doing trying to buy weapons in Brooklyn this morning?"

"I am a security agent for the family of my

president," Dominic said. He clenched his hands together between his knees. "Part of my job is to buy weapons to better do my duty."

Vaughn scoffed. "And as an agent of your government, you can't get these weapons through proper channels?"

Dominic rolled his eyes up toward Vaughn. "I don't deny it was not a smart move, but these men had items we cannot yet purchase in Italy. They were offering a good deal."

"So you expect me to believe that you were trying to purchase those guns in order to protect the first family," Vaughn said flatly.

"I don't expect you to believe anything," Dominic spat out. "I do not answer to you."

The tension between the two men heightened, and Vaughn stared Dominic in the eye, refusing to be the first to look away. The longer they stayed like that, however, the sillier Vaughn felt—like he was having a schoolyard standoff.

"Who was the woman at the pizzeria?" he asked finally, still not breaking his gaze.

"I have no idea," Dominic said, looking away again.

"She let you go?" Vaughn asked.

"Yes. When she chased you," Dominic said. He smiled slyly. "Thank you for that."

Vaughn pressed his lips together, then rested his knuckles on the table and leaned in to them. "You are aware that we have your partners in custody."

Dominic looked at him then, the color leaving his face. Vaughn struggled to keep from smiling at this stunned reaction. "My partners?" Dominic asked.

Vaughn opened the file and removed the pictures that had been taken of the suspects when they were brought in. He tossed each one onto the table, facing Dominic, as he said their names.

"Carlo Prizzi . . . Tomas Viana . . . Gianni Rinascente . . ."

Dominic slowly faced the table, gazing down at the photographs of the sneering, defiant men. He reached up with both hands and wiped his mouth dry. His fingers, Vaughn noticed, were trembling.

"These men have already admitted their roles in La Rappresaglia," Vaughn told him. "How long do you think it will be before they finger you?"

"Th-these men have . . . admitted . . . ?" Dominic stammered, his brow furrowing deeply. "*These* men?"

"They're guilty," Vaughn said, staring at Dominic. "And so are you."

Dominic slapped his hands down on the first

photo and pushed them all away from him. He glared up at Vaughn, his eyes suddenly moistening. "I have nothing more to say."

"You're going to be taken back to Italy," Vaughn told him, gathering the pictures again. "They'll deal with you on your own soil. Can you imagine the kind of welcome your people will give to a traitor like you?"

Dominic turned his back on Vaughn, this time for good. Vaughn glared at his hunched back, frustration mounting within him. This was not going well.

"If I were you, I'd think about talking," Vaughn told him. "We can't help you unless you cooperate."

His comment was met with stony silence. Vaughn sighed, put the file back together, and exited the room, slamming the door closed behind him. So much for the satisfaction of seeing Dominic's face fall when he realized the game was over. The guy wasn't giving an inch.

"No luck, huh?" Chloe asked, standing up from her computer. Vaughn knew she had watched everything on her monitor thanks to cameras positioned in the corners of the interrogation room.

"He's guilty," Vaughn said, handing the file back to her. "Did you see his reaction when he saw the faces of the men we'd brought in?"

Chloe tilted her head and bit her lip, knocking the fold of the file against her palm. "I don't know, Vaughn. We got IDs on those weapons dealers he was meeting with—the men anyway. They're very small time. You'd think La Rappresaglia would have better contacts than them."

"I think that makes total sense," Vaughn countered. "Why would they want to draw attention to themselves while they were here by meeting with more well-known dealers? They probably *wanted* to keep it small."

Chloe shrugged a shoulder and sat down again. Vaughn slumped into the chair across from hers. He rubbed his brow, thinking through the bizarre events of the day. There was something missing in all this. Some clue. Some key that was right in front of him. He could sense it.

"What about the woman at the pizzeria?" Vaughn asked, leaning forward.

"She's not one of ours. The camera never got a clear shot of her, but CIA maintains no other officers were on site. Our Italian counterparts confirmed that she doesn't work for Italy, either." Chloe glanced up from her computer screen long enough to shoot Vaughn a foreboding glance. "She must work for some foreign government or militia."

Vaughn blinked, taking in this news. "That

doesn't make any sense. She seemed like she was sent there to stop Dominic—to stop La Rappresaglia. Who else would send her to do that?"

Before either of them could venture a guess, the door behind Vaughn opened and President Toscana entered the room, flanked by his bodyguards. Chloe and Vaughn both stood. The president's face was a mask of anxiety as he crossed over to Vaughn. In all the newsreels and publicity stills Vaughn had seen of this man over the years, he'd never seen him appear quite so agitated.

"Agent Vaughn, I wanted to thank you personally for saving my daughter's life," Toscana said, extending his hand.

Overwhelmed, Vaughn reached out and clasped the president's hand. His heart suddenly overflowed with pride. "Just doing my job, sir," he said with a tight smile.

"I still cannot believe the extent of this conspiracy," the president said, shaking his head. "So many of my trusted men . . . . We're conducting interviews of the rest of our personnel, subjecting them to lie-detector tests. It is awful for them—for us—but what else can I do?"

"I'm sorry it had to happen this way, but at least we found out before they did any real harm," Vaughn said.

"Yes, well, I understand they claim that the threat still exists," the president said, his green eyes serious. "I hope that you will continue your post and keep watch over Marianna."

"Of course I will," Vaughn said, swallowing back even more pride. The president of Italy was asking him personally to take care of his only child. This didn't happen every day.

"Well, I will let you get back to work," Toscana said, nodding to Vaughn, then Chloe. "And thank you both again."

"You're welcome, Mr. President," Chloe said.

With that, President Toscana and his bodyguards swept out of the room.

"Well, that was nice," Chloe said.

For a moment, Vaughn thought of his father. Had he had moments like this? Heady moments, when men of great stature thanked him for a job well done? *I wish you were here to tell me, Dad,* Vaughn thought.

"You in there?" Chloe asked, startling him.

"Yeah, I—" Vaughn's cell phone trilled, cutting him off, and he reached into his breast pocket to grab it, shooting Chloe an apologetic glance.

"Agent Vaughn," he said, falling back into his chair.

"I just wanted to call and congratulate you on a job well done," Betty Harlow said.

"Uh . . . thank you, ma'am," Vaughn replied, shocked.

"Harlow?" Chloe mouthed.

"Just don't go getting a hero complex on me," Betty growled. "I can't tolerate that crap."

"No. Of course not."

"We'll see you in a couple of days," Betty said. "Pass my thanks on to Agent Murphy."

"I will," Vaughn replied.

He hung up the phone, placed it in his pocket, and leaned back in his chair, smiling at Chloe. She eyed him dubiously as he stretched out his legs and crooked his arms behind his head.

"Why do you look like that?" Chloe asked finally.

"Because Betty Harlow just called to personally congratulate me . . . well, *us,* on a job well done," he said.

Chloe sat down hard, her expression dazed. "Does she even *do* that?"

"She does now," Vaughn said, raising his eyebrows.

"Wow," Chloe said.

Vaughn took a deep breath and relaxed into the

chair, deciding to let himself enjoy this feeling of triumph, even if it was just for a few minutes. It wasn't every day that he received a personal thank-you from one of the most powerful and respected men in the world *and* a phone call from his boss, who wasn't known for her effusive expressions of praise.

"Okay, that's enough of that," Chloe said, breaking into his thoughts. "We still have Toscana's big speech at the UN tomorrow night, and don't forget there's an assassin on the loose."

"Right," Vaughn said, sitting up and placing his feet flat on the ground. The moment had passed, and in the real world he still had a job to do. "Back to work."

10

"WHO ARE WE GOING to meet at this place?" Vaughn asked Marianna as their limo zipped uptown later that night. He kept his eyes trained out the window at the lights of the city, the dog walkers and nannies and the trench-coated men and women rushing home from work.

There was nothing of particular interest for him outside the car, but focusing on the sidewalk prevented him from staring at Marianna's bare legs. She was wearing an extremely sexy fringed dress with a hemline that was almost X-rated. Somehow her delicately crossed ankles seemed to be inching closer and closer to him with each passing city block. Avoiding all contact, Vaughn had his elbow crooked on the door's arm rest, and his knees were turned away from Marianna. If she got any closer, he was going to have to jump out of the moving limo.

"They're just friends of mine from boarding school," Marianna replied blithely. "They go to Columbia, so I promised them I would meet up with them when I was in town."

"Friends? I don't know how much I trust your friends at this point," Vaughn said, only half kidding.

When Marianna didn't reply, he finally risked a glance in her direction and found her staring down at her lap. She fiddled with the small beaded purse in her hands and sighed, her expression dark.

Nice one, Vaughn. Very charming, he berated himself.

"I'm sorry," he told her. "I can't believe I just said that. I'm such an idiot."

He watched her fingers working as she twisted one black bead on the bag's strap around and around.

"No, *I'm* the idiot," she said, shaking her head. "You must think I'm so stupid. First Carlos and

Roberto, and now Dominic . . . Maybe my father's right. Maybe I am still a naïve child."

Vaughn reached out and placed his hand over Marianna's. "You're not a child," he said. "Look what you survived this morning."

Marianna scoffed and pulled her hand away, tucking it under her arm. "Oh, yes, I was very brave with all the screaming and crying," she said.

"You did fine," Vaughn replied. "Better than most people would have done. Believe me, I know."

Marianna looked at him tentatively, her face half in shadow, half illuminated by a streetlight outside her window. "Thank you for saying that."

"Well, it's true," Vaughn said.

He knew he was in trouble. He couldn't believe he'd actually put his hand on hers. What kind of CIA officer did that? One who was starting to fall for his assignment, that was what kind. He found himself looking forward to meeting Marianna's friends, even if they did turn out to be of the shallow, self-interested sort she'd surrounded herself with at the club the night before. At least with a few more people in the mix there would be no more loaded private moments.

The limousine swung around a corner and eased to a stop in front of a brick building with a long red awning stretching out to the edge of the sidewalk.

"This is it. Marcel's," the driver said.

Vaughn jumped out of the car and walked around to open the door for Marianna. As they made their way up the front steps, Vaughn slipped into work mode, keeping his eyes peeled for shadowy figures, men lurking in corners, anything remotely out of the ordinary. A tuxedoed man held the door open for them and smiled.

"Ms. Toscana," he said with a nod.

Vaughn tensed slightly. That was odd. Unless the guy was a serious student of current world events, why would the doorman at a restaurant on the Upper West Side know Marianna's name? Vaughn studied the man's angular face, committing it to memory, just in case. When the man stepped aside, Vaughn finally noticed it—something *very* out of the ordinary. There was no one in the restaurant. No one aside from a few members of the wait staff lined up along the right wall. All the tables were set with ivory tablecloths and china, candles flickered along the walls and on every available surface, but the place was deathly silent.

"What's going on?" Vaughn asked. This was one of the most popular eateries in the city. When he had told Elena where he and Marianna were headed, she'd looked it up online and found that even on weeknights it was next to impossible to get a reservation there. Where was everybody?

"You were so worried about my security," Marianna said to him as the maitre d' slipped her wrap from her shoulders. "So I reserved the entire restaurant." She smiled. "It reminds me of one of my favorite restaurants in Rome, Trattoria di Nardi. You should go there sometime."

Vaughn swallowed hard as he looked around at the polished wood chairs, the gleaming silver. He wasn't used to being caught off guard. "Your friends aren't coming, are they?"

"Michael, Michael, Michael," Marianna said, slipping her arms around one of his. "Those friends don't exist. When are you going to catch up?"

A hot, embarrassed, somewhat flattered blush covered Vaughn's face. "Marianna, we can't do this," he said gently. "We can't go out on a date."

"Are the lady and gentleman ready for their table?" the maitre d' asked, appearing soundlessly at their side. He was a slim man with slick black hair and a square face. Something about his smile made it clear to Vaughn that he enjoyed being in charge for an important guest like Marianna.

"It's just dinner, Michael," Marianna said, biting her lip. Suddenly she looked vulnerable again, less in charge than she had just moments ago. Vaughn realized that she'd given him the power to hurt her. He hated it when women did that. It almost always made him crumble.

It is *just dinner, as long as you keep it casual,* Vaughn told himself. *Just get it over with.*

"Okay," he said with a sigh, cracking a small smile that caused Marianna to grin. "We have to eat, right?"

"This way," the maitre d' said, bowing before he started to wind his way around the deserted tables and chairs toward the back of the room. He had been loitering nearby while Marianna and Vaughn conversed, obviously waiting to pounce the second a decision was made.

Vaughn walked behind Marianna, watching the swish of the fringe on the hem of her black dress as she walked—watching her hips sway slowly back and forth. The moment he realized what he was doing, he blushed again and averted his eyes, forcing himself to recheck the perimeter of the restaurant. If he didn't get control of his hormones, he was never going to make it through this night.

"Our finest table," the maitre d' said, pulling a chair out for Marianna.

The table was stationed in the corner behind the

privacy of an old-fashioned accordion-style room divider. Vaughn realized it was probably there to afford solitude for romance-seeking couples, but considering romance was not on the agenda and there were no other diners in the restaurant, its presence was pointless. And the screen obscured his view of the room. He folded it up to the wall, ignoring the tongue clucking of the maitre d'.

"Is the table unacceptable, sir?" the man asked.

"No. The table is just fine."

Vaughn took the corner seat across from Marianna and surveyed the restaurant. From where he sat he had a view of the front door, the bathrooms, and the kitchen door. No one would enter the room without Vaughn's seeing them.

A tall man sat down at a grand piano on the other side of the restaurant near the deserted bar and began to play a jazz tune at a quiet, unobtrusive volume. Marianna smiled at Vaughn, her eyes shining in the candlelight as the maitre d' slipped a pair of menus in front of them. Vaughn felt a very first-date-like stirring in his chest and wondered what Betty would say if she could see him now.

"Snap out of it, Lothario," he heard her voice say in his ear. *"Who do you think you are?"*

"If you would like the soufflé for dessert, I

suggest you put in your order now," the maitre d'
said, folding his hands together at waist level as he
loomed over the table.

"I don't think we'll be staying for dessert,"
Vaughn said, attempting to get back to a busi-
nesslike atmosphere.

"Michael, there's no rush," Marianna said,
peeking over her menu. She locked eyes with him
and lowered her chin. "After all, we do have all
night."

Something in the way she said it made
Vaughn's heart stir again. *All night.* All night with
Marianna. His nonagent side—the side he was not
supposed to be listening to—very much liked the
sound of that. He glanced around the room and
checked his watch. It was only eight o'clock. He'd
told Chloe he would be out for the night with Marianna and her friends, figuring he'd probably end up
at another downtown club standing in the corner
while they partied. His partner would never know
that the evening had turned out differently.

No one would know—unless he decided to tell
them.

Marianna gazed at him steadily across the
table, her eyes challenging him to break the rules.
There was just something about her. Something

mysterious—something intriguing. Something that made it so easy to forget everything else.

"The soufflé sounds great," Vaughn told the maitre d'. He exchanged a slow smile with Marianna, savoring the thrill of his racing pulse. "And we'd like to take a look at the wine list as well."

*   *   *

"It's beautiful here, isn't it?" Marianna leaned her forearms on the iron fence that overlooked the Hudson River and the New Jersey coastline on the opposite shore. It was a cool, clear night, and the lights on the buildings across the way glinted in the darkness like thousands of low-flying stars. During the day the same buildings were gray, industrial blocks of brick, but at night there was something romantic about the view.

Vaughn studied Marianna's profile, dozens of cheesy movie lines flitting through his mind unbidden. *The view's beautiful from where* I'm *standing. . . . It's even more beautiful because of you. . . .* He cleared his throat and turned away, resisting the urge to say something he would regret on every conceivable level.

"It's too exposed out here," he told her, leaning

back against the fence. He scanned the walkways of Riverside Park, unable to distinguish the faces of the joggers and pedestrians in the darkness. "We should really get you back to the hotel."

Marianna sighed, a breeze tossing her dark curls around her face. She tipped her head forward and stared down at the rippling water. Vaughn had a feeling he knew what was coming—she wanted to talk. All night she had been trying to find out more about him, trying to inject a romantic vibe into the dinner by feeding him from her fork and touching his hand on the table. Vaughn had done everything he could to deflect her advances without being outright rude, but he could tell from Marianna's tentative body language that she was about to call him on it.

The locale she had chosen for this talk wasn't lost on him either. It was Marianna who had suggested a stroll through the park, ending down by the water. There was no better setting for a goodnight kiss between two people who couldn't, under any circumstances, go back to one another's rooms at the hotel. Though neither of them said this aloud, they both knew it all too well.

"Did you have a good time tonight?" Marianna asked, tossing her hair over her shoulder as she turned her head to face him.

"I did," Vaughn replied truthfully. It had been

more than good. In the moments he had let his guard down, it had been fun and interesting and very datelike. Then the guilt would seep in and the good feeling would end until he found himself slipping again. He'd spent the evening on an internal roller coaster.

"Really? Because you've seemed a little . . . closed off," Marianna said, standing up straight. She pulled her wrap more tightly around her slim shoulders and searched his face, waiting for him to explain.

Vaughn sighed. "Marianna . . . I *have* to be closed off," Vaughn said, pushing his hands into the pockets of his gray trench coat. "I'm supposed to be protecting you. I can't . . . get distracted."

A sexy smile slid across her face and she stepped closer to him. "Is there something about me that you find distracting?"

He watched her hand reaching out for him, knowing he should stop her, but somehow he was frozen. When she rested her hand on his cheek, the warmth of her touch seemed to spread throughout his entire body. The heady scent of her perfume filled his senses, pushing him closer and closer to the edge.

How had he let this happen? How had he let himself start falling for this person he had despised just yesterday—the last person in the world he should even be thinking about? She was too young for him. She lived in another country. She was the daughter of a dignitary. And to top it all off, he had a responsibility to take care of her. Mixing business with pleasure wasn't just frowned upon by the CIA—it was forbidden.

"Marianna," Vaughn said, his throat dry. "I can't—"

"Michael, if you don't kiss me right now, I'm going to throw myself into the river and you are going to be in big trouble with your boss."

Vaughn's heart skipped a beat, and before he knew what he was doing, he'd slipped his hands under the thick blanket of her hair.

"I guess I can't argue with that," he mumbled.

She closed her eyes and tipped her face toward his. Vaughn leaned down and touched his lips to hers. It had been years since he had experienced a first kiss with someone, and he'd forgotten about the rush, the fog that took over his brain. As Marianna wrapped her arms around him and pressed her body closer to his, the voices in his mind faded to nothing and his racing heart took over.

For the moment, Agent Vaughn was breaking all the rules, but Michael was exactly where he was supposed to be.

11

VAUGHN ESCORTED THE TOSCANA family back to the presidential suite along with a half-dozen Italian security personnel, some of whom had been called to duty in the States after their colleagues had been taken into custody. As he followed the line of dark-suited men, Vaughn felt as conspicuous as a professional hockey player with no missing teeth. The new security people had been cold to him all morning, unable to decide whether he was the enemy, for bringing down their friends, or their friend, for bringing down their enemies.

Meanwhile, he felt as if Marianna's parents

could see right through him, as if they were completely aware of the struggle he'd been enduring all morning. They knew why he'd been avoiding eye contact with Marianna, why he'd practically flinched when she'd grabbed his arm for balance getting out of the limousine at the UN that morning. Marianna, of course, seemed to be going out of her way to be as close to Vaughn as possible even as he avoided it, making his defensive tactics all the more conspicuous. He felt like a teenager suffering under the evil eye of his prom date's parents. Every time he caught Mrs. Toscana looking in his direction, he was certain he could read disapproval on her dark features. His guilty conscience was sure that Marianna had told her everything.

They're going to have me taken off the case, Vaughn thought, sweating underneath his tight shirt collar. *They're going to call Betty and tell her all about my unprofessional conduct, and I'm going to be a laughingstock at Langley.*

Vaughn took his place near the wall, behind the couch on which Marianna and her mother had seated themselves, running his finger between his collar and his neck. There was a heavy silence over the room as everyone mulled over the horrifying statistics they had heard that morning. The family had attended a breakfast at the UN, followed by a symposium on the world AIDS crisis. From the lack of conversation in the limo on the way back to the hotel, virtually everyone had been affected by the speakers, the video footage, the overwhelming facts.

And here I am stressing about a schoolboy's crush, Vaughn thought, shaking his head. *What is wrong with me? No one else here is thinking about me and Marianna.*

"Agent Vaughn, how do you feel about my daughter?" Mrs. Toscana asked suddenly.

Vaughn's heart leaped out of his mouth and hit the floor at his feet. All eyes in the room turned to focus on him, and once again, he imagined that they could all read the guilt scrawled across his face. Vaughn glanced at Marianna, whose eyes were wide. Suddenly he realized that his breathing was unusually loud.

"I . . . I'm sorry. . . . What was the question?" Vaughn asked, taking a couple of shaky steps toward the family. He fought for his good old CIA composure but found it curiously lacking in the face of disapproving parents.

"I believe what my wife is trying to ask is how would you feel about spending this last day with

Marianna?" President Toscana explained. He stood up from his chair and went over to the wet bar, where he poured himself a tall glass of water from a silver pitcher. "Her mother and I have meetings to attend all day, and since it is Marianna's last day in New York, we were hoping you wouldn't mind escorting her around the city. I'm sure there are still a few sights she would like to see."

Vaughn knew he couldn't turn the president down. It was his assignment, after all—he was to stick by Marianna's side. But after what had happened between them the night before, he'd spent hours berating himself for his behavior and promising himself nothing more would happen. He had believed that the day would be spent with her family and thought he would be safe from temptation. This new development was not good.

Marianna and her mother and father all stared at Vaughn as if he were an escaped lunatic, waiting for the answer they knew he was obligated to give.

"Agent Vaughn?" President Toscana prompted.

Vaughn snapped back to attention. Well, if they were going to *force* him . . . He took a deep breath, looked at Marianna, and gave her a lopsided smile. Her features instantly relaxed and she smiled back.

"Of course," Vaughn said. "I would be happy to take Marianna wherever she'd like to go."

* * *

"I can't believe of all the restaurants in this city, you want to eat here," Vaughn said with a laugh. He stepped away from the door at the Second Avenue Deli to let an elderly couple pass. The small deli was bustling with people clamoring for attention at the counter and crowding around the chrome tables that seemed to be right on top of one another. The acrid scents of frying grease, strong coffee, and sour pickles mingled in the air to create a unique aroma.

"They're supposed to have the best pastrami in the world," Marianna said as the hostess snapped her fingers in the air to get their attention. Marianna followed the woman to a table smack in the center of the restaurant. Vaughn had to walk on tiptoe and turn to the side to maneuver past the men at the next table.

"I don't take you as a pastrami type of girl," Vaughn said as he sat. He pulled his arms in close to his body to avoid bumping into the hulking guy to his left and the diminutive woman to his right. Quarters were so tight he didn't even bother to attempt coat removal.

"I'm not as predictable as you seem to think," Marianna said, raising one eyebrow at him. She effortlessly slipped out of her black jacket, letting it fall over the back of her chair.

Vaughn's pulse skittered under her flirtatious gaze, and he smiled. If she wanted to pretend she was mysterious, he would play along, but the more time he spent with Marianna, the more he felt he already knew her. She was a fun-loving, risk-taking, spoiled rich girl who was used to getting what she wanted. But she also cared about her family and her country and had a vulnerable side that showed itself every so often—a side he was grateful to have seen.

"What'll ya have?" a harried-looking waitress asked, pulling a pencil from behind her ear as she approached the table.

"Two pastrami sandwiches with extra pickles," Marianna said before Vaughn could open his mouth.

"You got it, toots," the waitress said, grabbing their grease-spotted menus.

"Oh, so now you're ordering for me?" Vaughn asked.

Marianna sat forward, resting both elbows on the table. "Like I said, I'm unpredictable," she told him.

"You don't even know if I like pastrami," Vaughn said.

"Don't you?"

"I don't know. I've never had it," Vaughn admitted, leaning back in his chair.

"What? Are you insane?" Marianna blurted out, earning a few irritated glances from their neighbors. "Well, you are going to thank me."

Vaughn smiled at her indignation and realized he hadn't stopped smiling for more than five seconds all morning. Playing Marianna's body guard was getting to be more like a vacation than a mission.

"Sheesh, Michael, you only live once," Marianna said, fiddling with her napkin. "And only for so long."

Vaughn's heart thumped and his face fell. He reached across the table and took Marianna's hand, this time not allowing himself the internal debate that had preceded all earlier touching. Marianna glanced up at him but then quickly looked away.

"I'm not going to let anything happen to you," he told her, squeezing her palm. "We got the bad guys, remember? You're safe."

As far as Vaughn knew, no one had told Marianna about the bodyguards' claim that the assassin assigned to take out her father was still at large. It was a fact everyone agreed she didn't need to know.

"For now," Marianna said quietly as the waitress deposited two heaping platters of food on their table.

Vaughn realized for the first time exactly how profound an effect the last few days had had on Marianna. When he had first graduated from the Farm, the danger he faced every day had affected his dreams for weeks. It had been difficult to sleep and eat and think like a normal human being. All that had faded for him now, but it wasn't so easy for a regular person to get over.

"Hey, we're supposed to be having fun today, remember?" Vaughn said, looking down at the hulking sandwich on his plate. "Although I might need you to rush me to the hospital for a bypass after this."

Marianna laughed. "Come on, try it," she said.

"That's a lot of meat," Vaughn said, picking up the huge sandwich with both hands.

"If you finish it, I'll let you pick our next activity," Marianna told him, her eyes dancing.

"Really?" Vaughn said teasingly. "You sure about that?"

"Absolutely," Marianna shot back. Her expression told him that there was nothing he could suggest that could intimidate her.

We'll see about that, Vaughn thought. He took a huge bite of his sandwich and his mouth exploded with the tangy, smoky taste.

"Oh . . . wow," he said, his mouth full.

"See? I told you," Marianna said, lifting her

hand toward him. "You haven't lived until you've tasted pastrami."

* * *

There was no sound in the world that Vaughn loved more than sharpened blades slicing against freshly Zambonied ice. He tipped his head back, letting the breeze created by his speed whip past his face as he took another lap around the perimeter of the ice at Wollman Rink. The skating facility in Central Park was packed, as always, with kids and tourists and packs of teenagers, many of them amateurs who lost their footing every five feet and hit the ground in tangles of limbs and scarves and cameras. They all recognized the odd expert when they saw him, and many of them were watching Vaughn, slipping out of his way whenever he zipped by.

While most of the skaters were keeping an eye on their feet, Vaughn was keeping an eye on Marianna. She was standing at the edge of the rink, clinging to the railing while trying to look nonchalant. Every time he passed her, she swore she was going to get on the ice the next time he came around. So far he'd done five laps.

"All right, that's it," Vaughn said, kicking up a sprinkling of snowy dust as he stopped in front of her. "Are you really telling me that you've never ice-skated before?"

"Not never," Marianna said, her ankles wobbling as she stood up straight. "Just not since I was six years old."

"It'll come back to you," Vaughn said, holding out his arms. "Come on."

"Why did I let you talk me into this?" Marianna said with a smile. She stepped toward him and clutched his elbows.

"Hey, you said if I finished my sandwich—"

"How was I supposed to know you could eat something that size?" Marianna asked. "Your waist is smaller than mine."

"Yeah. Not quite," Vaughn replied, checking out her tiny midsection. "Okay. Are you ready?"

"I suppose."

Vaughn skated back a few feet, pulling Marianna across the ice. She leaned all her weight on him, bending forward at the waist, staring at her feet. As she inched forward, she tried to stand up straight, but Vaughn felt her pulling back, falling backward. Every time she lost her balance slightly, her grip on him tightened a bit more.

"I feel like a complete incompetent," Marianna said to the ice.

"You're doing fine," Vaughn said, glancing

over his shoulder to make sure he wasn't about to skate them both into a wall. "Try to look up. Look where you're going instead of concentrating on your feet."

Marianna did as she was told and rolled her shoulders back, staring into Vaughn's eyes. For a moment, Vaughn let himself gaze back at her. All the screeching, laughing, flailing skaters around them grew muted and dull. Vaughn's heart raced.

Then she fell.

"Ah!" Marianna shouted, her feet going out from under her.

Vaughn grasped her arms and caught her before she could hit the ice. He bent at the knees, gripping her awkwardly, suspending her a few inches from the cold, grainy surface.

"Don't let go!" Marianna said through her laughter. "If you let me go I'll have to kill you."

"I gotcha," Vaughn said, laughing as well. He pulled her up awkwardly, his skates sliding around while her feet flailed crazily, trying to find solid footing.

"Okay, that was embarrassing," Marianna said, straightening her jacket as she stood, one arm still gripping Vaughn.

"You know, you were right. You really are bad at this," Vaughn told her.

Marianna squinted at him. "Maybe you're just a bad teacher."

"Is that a challenge?" Vaughn retorted.

"I don't know," Marianna said, lifting her shoulders. "I just think that if I had the proper instruction I wouldn't be falling on my butt."

"All right, that's it." Vaughn said, turning so he was standing next to her. "By the end of this day, you will be an expert."

Marianna grinned and hooked her arm through his. For the next half hour, Vaughn gave her every instruction and tip he had ever received when he was a boy first learning how to skate. He taught her how to keep her feet under her, how to lean forward only slightly to keep her balance, how to push off with her toe. Marianna almost hit the deck a couple more times, but Vaughn always caught her. By the time the ice closed down for its scheduled Zamboni break, Marianna was able to skate halfway around the perimeter without clinging to Vaughn.

"Maybe you are a good teacher," Marianna said as they stepped off the ice.

"You're a quick study," Vaughn told her.

"So, what do we do next?" Marianna asked, wobbling inside to the crowded locker area.

Vaughn checked his watch and was surprised to see how late it had gotten. "We should actually head back," he said. "You need to get ready for the event tonight, and I need to be debriefed."

Marianna leaned back against the end of a row of lockers. She sighed and cast her gaze to the ground. "It's almost over," she said. She caught Vaughn's quizzical glance. "My trip to the States."

Vaughn knew Marianna was going home tomorrow, but with everything else that had been going on in the past few days, he hadn't had time to think about what that actually meant. She was going home—and he would probably never see her again.

"Well, this is a fun moment," Marianna said, breaking the morose silence. "I'm going to go to the ladies' room."

"I'll come with," he said.

"Of course you will," Marianna replied with a smile.

She sat down on the bench, took off her skates, and changed back into her boots. Vaughn changed quickly as well and followed her to the end of the hallway that led to the bathrooms. Keeping an eye on the door, he waited by the corner while she went inside.

There was a heaviness in Vaughn's chest that he couldn't explain away. The idea of Marianna's departure had hit him harder than he could have imagined. How had this happened in two short days?

Vaughn stood up straight when Marianna emerged from the ladies' room. At the same moment a tall man with brown, close-cropped hair came out of the men's room across the way. He was wearing a red parka and jeans and looked just like every other father roaming around the place, but something about him felt familiar to Vaughn, and the hair on the back of his neck stood up. As Marianna pushed her arms into her jacket, she dropped her scarf, and the tall man bent to pick it up for her. Vaughn instantly started forward, but a group of toddling kids blocked his way. Marianna smiled and thanked the man, and the two exchanged a few words—from what Vaughn could see, it looked like standard pleasantries, but he could hear nothing over the din in the locker room. Finally the man stepped away from Marianna, getting lost in the crowd just as Vaughn arrived at her side. He attempted to get a good look at the tall man's face, but he turned away before Vaughn could study his features.

"Everything okay?" Vaughn asked, watching the man's back as he retreated.

"Fine," Marianna said. She looped the scarf around her neck and smiled. "Ready to go?"

"Yeah. Let's get you back to your parents," Vaughn said. Only when the man was well out of sight did Vaughn's muscles start to relax. The goose bumps that had formed along his arms began to subside.

"Oh, yay," Marianna said sarcastically.

Vaughn forced a smile and started for the door. Something about that man had set him off, and now all he wanted was to get Marianna back to the hotel, where there would be dozens of people watching over her. He would never admit it aloud, but considering the way he'd been feeling all day, the way his thoughts had constantly strayed from his purpose, he was no longer sure he was the best person to be protecting Marianna. In that respect, it was a good thing this mission was almost over.

Marianna reached down and entwined her fingers with his, giving his hand a squeeze that was echoed in his chest.

In every other respect, he wished this mission would never end.

* * *

"We have a new lead," Chloe told Vaughn the moment he stepped into HQ at the hotel. She crossed the room holding a slim stack of eight-by-ten photos and handed them to him. Elena and Barry both swiveled around in their chairs to catch his reaction to the breakthrough.

Vaughn shrugged out of his jacket, transferring the pictures from one hand to another. They were photos of a car lot taken from an overhead angle— probably a security camera positioned on the dealership building. Multicolored flags lined the parking lot, and each car windshield was emblazoned with a special offer in neon paint: DRIVE ME HOME TODAY! ONLY $500 DOWN!

"Okay, what's the lead?" Vaughn asked.

"We traced the vans the kidnappers used back to this car lot in Edison, New Jersey," Chloe explained, tapping the photo with the eraser end of her pencil. "Look at the next one."

Vaughn flipped the top picture to the back. The next shot featured two men standing in the lot near a black van—definitely one of the vehicles used in the kidnapping. The shorter man wore a tie under his jacket and was clearly the salesman. The other wore a black leather jacket and was partially turned away from the camera. A frizzy ponytail hovered just above the back of his collar.

Vaughn went to the next photo. In this one, the man's face was more visible. He was wearing sunglasses, but there was no doubt in his mind of who the man was. He'd seen him just two nights ago, standing at the bar at Trick, right next to the blond arms dealer and his mystery woman.

"Do you have these on the computer?" Vaughn asked, glancing at Elena.

"Yep." She popped open a window on her screen, and the three photos appeared in thumbnail size.

"Enhance this one for me," Vaughn said, pointing at the last photo.

"Vaughn, have you seen this guy?" Chloe asked as they hovered over Elena's shoulders. Barry stood up as well, jockeying for a view as Elena enlarged the photo.

"Can you zoom in on his chin?" Vaughn asked, reaching around Elena to tap the screen.

"You got it," she said.

Before Vaughn's eyes the photo blurred and widened, then slowly grew more and more crisp. As the image focused, Vaughn's blood ran cold. It was there, just as he had known it would be—a small, X-shaped scar right on the left side of the man's chin.

And now that he was staring at the man's face, Vaughn realized something even more horrifying: That night at the club was not the only time he had seen this man. The very same guy had been right in front of him that afternoon, just inches from Marianna. He'd cut his hair and changed his clothes, but this was definitely the man that had retrieved

Marianna's scarf for her at the rink just an hour ago. Vaughn had stood there and watched while one of Marianna's kidnappers had brushed fingertips with her.

Vaughn threw the photographs down on the table and turned away from the computer, unable to look at the evidence of his failure.

"Vaughn! What is it?" Chloe demanded.

"This guy was at the club two nights ago," Vaughn told her, shame seeping into his veins. "And today . . . today he actually spoke to Marianna, right in front of me."

Vaughn clenched his jaw as he watched Chloe's face fall. He knew what she was thinking, because he was thinking the exact same thing. He'd failed on one of the simplest missions he could have ever asked for.

He took a deep breath and looked his partner in the eye, calling up every ounce of effort to admit the truth to her and to himself.

"This man has been stalking Marianna and me for two days . . . and I didn't even notice."

12

VAUGHN STEPPED OUT OF the elevator and walked down the hallway toward Marianna's room, cursing his own incompetence. Just yesterday he'd been preening over his success, letting his head swell over Betty's phone call and President Toscana's thanks. What had he given them in return for their confidence and pride? Total obliviousness.

At least we know now, Vaughn thought. *It's not too late to catch this guy.* But first on his list of priorities was making sure Marianna was okay. Once her safety was secured, he would find out what the suspect had said to her earlier at the rink. A man who got that close to his mark in a public place was getting sloppy. He was getting desperate. Maybe he'd slipped up and said something that could give Vaughn a clue to his identity or his whereabouts.

Vaughn went around the corner, took one look at the door to Marianna's room, and stopped. The hallway was empty. There were no guards stationed at Marianna's door. The absence of their hulking bodies made the wide hall feel like a black hole. Vaughn was filled with a dark, poisonous fear.

What had happened to the guards? Why had they deserted their post? Were they also agents of La Rappresaglia who had somehow slipped under the radar? And if so, did they already have Marianna?

If she'd been taken again, Vaughn had no one to blame but himself.

Vaughn drew his gun from his holster and started toward the door, stepping as lightly as possible. With his back against the wall right next to the door, Vaughn reached out his right arm and carefully, quietly, tried the doorknob. He held his breath, not sure what to hope for.

The doorknob turned in his grasp, unlocked. Not a good sign. Vaughn opened the door a crack, pressing his eyes closed as a rivulet of sweat ran down the side of his face. He had to stay calm to face whatever or whoever might be inside that room.

Just let her be alive, he thought. *Please just let her be alive.*

Vaughn turned and pushed through the door, holding his gun at shoulder level, half expecting to be jumped by two huge guards. Instead, Marianna turned to look at him, surprised, from across the room. Instantly Vaughn relaxed. She was here and she was fine. She was standing next to the small dining table in a glittering ball gown, her makeup done, her hair swept up, and she was fine.

For a split second, Vaughn experience unadulterated relief. Then his brain slowly took in the details.

Marianna was standing with her foot resting on the seat of a chair, strapping something to her thigh with invisible tape.

Vaughn's stomach churned.

It was a gun.

"Marianna, what's going on?" Vaughn asked, his mouth dry as bone.

She lowered her foot to the floor and gazed at him, a mixture of triumph and sympathy in her eyes. Vaughn felt the sickening sensation of betrayal—felt it all over his skin. He was repulsed by the glimmer of condescension on her face as well. It was as if she was mocking him—mocking him for how easy it had been to scam him.

Vaughn took in the rest of the room. Two guards slumped against the wall, unconscious, probably dead. He saw the blood trickling down the side of one of their necks, soaking the white fabric of his collar—saw the unnatural angle at which the other man's arm hung to the floor.

Sweet, vulnerable, fun-loving Marianna had killed her own bodyguards.

"I don't understand," Vaughn said, not *wanting* to understand.

"I'm the assassin, Michael," Marianna said, taking a few steps toward him, the silken fabric of her dress swishing as she walked. "I'm the bad guy."

This isn't possible, Vaughn thought, desperately clinging to a lie. *Not Marianna.*

She took another step closer to him, and Vaughn's survival instinct kicked in. He mustered up all his strength to fight against the emotions swirling through his heart, lifted his gun, and trained it directly on Marianna's beautiful face— the face he'd daydreamed about holding and kissing goodbye later this evening.

"Don't move," Vaughn told her. "You're going to have to come with me."

"I don't think so," Marianna said. Her eyes flicked up and over his shoulder, telling Vaughn that there was someone behind him. He began to turn, but it was too late. Something large and heavy hit him on the back of his head. The last thing he saw before blacking out was the smirk on Marianna's soft, perfect lips.

*   *   *

Vaughn's first sensation was that of blinding pain. His head throbbed whenever he moved, whenever he blinked, whenever he took a breath. His arms were suspended above him, linked together with a pair of metal cuffs, and his shoulders ached from strain. He realized as he came to that he must have been hanging like this for a few minutes in order for his arms to feel like dead weight. A loud, roaring sound reverberated in his ears and surrounded him, coming from all sides. Some kind of heavy machinery was running nearby. From the intensity of the volume, he would have guessed it was a plane engine, but that wasn't possible, was it?

"He's waking up," a male voice said nearby.

Vaughn opened his eyes and two figures hovering over him came into focus. He saw the glittering colors of Marianna's gown swim before his vision. The scent of her perfume filled his nostrils.

"Agent Vaughn," the man said, moving closer, coming in to sharper focus. "We meet at last."

Vaughn stared at the X-shaped scar on the man's chin, and the sight of it made something inside him snap. He shook himself awake, pain radiating from the lump on the back of his head, and scanned his surroundings. He was in a large room with harsh white walls that were peppered with cracks. Soft white sacks were piled up and spilled from rolling bins, each with a pink tag dangling from its closure. A row of industrial-sized washing machines lined the wall behind his captors, flanked by a row of dryers, which were creating the deafening noise.

They were in the hotel's laundry room. Vaughn looked up and found that his wrists were cuffed to a huge metal shelf packed with bottles of detergent and fabric softener and piles upon piles of towels and sheets. He struggled to his feet, wincing as his shoulders adjusted, his knees unlocking from the position they'd been crooked into on the floor.

"Who are you?" Vaughn asked the man, gritting his teeth against the pain.

The man smiled slowly and stepped away from Vaughn. He stood next to Marianna, and together Vaughn's kidnappers faced him.

"Don't you see the resemblance, Michael?" Marianna asked. "This is my brother, Emilio. The founder of La Rappresaglia."

"I'm the founder, but she's the real leader,"

Emilio said, reaching out to squeeze Marianna's shoulder like a proud brother. "Mari is the brains of the family."

Vaughn's blood ran cold. He studied their faces. There was no denying they were related—the square jawline, the deep-set eyes. When Emilio's hair was long, it had had the same wild curls that Marianna's had now. Still, something inside Vaughn resisted. It just couldn't be.

"President Toscana doesn't have a son," he countered.

"Or so the world believes," Emilio said, a shadow of anger passing over his features—a shadow Vaughn recognized. It had transformed Marianna's features just two nights ago when he had mentioned her only-child status. Suddenly Vaughn understood the anger he'd seen on her face then. She was not an only child—that was just a lie her father let the world believe. But somehow, Marianna had found the truth.

"You see, I was illegitimate. The product of one drunken night the young future president had in Sicily thirty years ago," Emilio explained. "My mother told him he was going to be a father and he rejected her. He was a statesman, bound for great things. She was nothing but a poor factory worker's daughter. He could not be connected to her. To me."

"When Emilio first contacted me a few years ago, I couldn't believe it," Marianna put in, looking up at her brother. "I couldn't believe my father could ever do anything as cold as abandoning a child. But it all checked out, Michael. We had tests done and the results were definitive. Emilio is my brother."

"And he's the one who asked you to join La Rappresaglia," Vaughn said, everything falling into place.

La Rappresaglia wasn't a revolutionary movement, it was a kid trying to get back at his deadbeat father.

"I'm sorry I lied to you, Michael," Marianna said, walking over to him. "I know that I owe you an explanation, so if there is anything you want to ask me, this is your chance. What do you want to know?"

Vaughn stared back at her, wishing she would get out of his sight. Looking at her reminded him of how stupid he'd been, how gullible. She'd played the poor-little-rich-girl routine on him, and he'd bitten. She'd talked about how concerned she was for her father, how he didn't deserve to die, and Vaughn had swallowed it whole.

Now he was trapped in the basement. Marianna was going to leave him here, go to the UN, and kill her own father, and there was nothing he could do about it. By this time next week he'd be chained to a desk, pushing papers for the duration of his career at the CIA.

If he lived that long.

"I see," Marianna said. "You're too proud to ask questions. But I'll tell you anyway."

She crossed her arms over her chest, holding them to her for warmth, and paced in front of him, her high heels clicking against the concrete floor.

"First, the kidnapping," Marianna began, looking at her feet as she walked. "I knew you were a smart man, Michael. I knew it the moment I met you. I wasn't sure if even I was going to be able to convince you that I was an innocent, ignorant girl. So we engineered the kidnapping to throw you off. The men you captured were not some of my best." She paused and looked him dead in the eye. "I assume they cracked within five minutes of being in custody."

Vaughn looked away, basically confirming this. His mind worked over the kidnapping carefully. It all made sense now: why there had been so few men guarding them with so few weapons, why their escape had been fairly easy. Vaughn had realized at the time that the men were bad shots and counted himself lucky for it. Now he realized that they were probably *trying* to miss. They didn't want to take out their boss, after all. They couldn't kill the assassin who was here to achieve their ultimate goal.

"He's your father," Vaughn heard himself say. "How can you kill your own father?"

Emilio scoffed, but Vaughn ignored him. He felt a lump form in his throat over his own words. He would give anything to have his father back again, even if it were just for one day. His murder still kept Vaughn up some nights, tossing and turning and wishing there were something he could have done.

"He is an enemy of the people," Marianna said flatly, her eyes seeming to darken. "*My* people. They are supposed to be his people, but he does not care for them. All he cares for is his own pocketbook—his own glory. I shudder when I think about how ignorant I was before Emilio came into my life."

She smiled slightly at Emilio, and his dark eyes glittered. *Evil,* Vaughn thought. *Pure evil.* This guy had brainwashed Marianna, plain and simple.

"Emilio taught me about the neighborhood where he grew up and the hundreds of other neighborhoods like it," Marianna continued passionately. "There are people in my country, good people, who are out of work and starving, and yet my father takes his private jet all over the world to visit his friends, go deep-sea fishing off the coast of Australia, play golf with your president in North Carolina. His government jails men who steal to feed their families and lets wealthy business owners who embezzle money from their employees go free. Entire neighborhoods are crumbling while government money goes to building schools for the rich. The man is not worthy of his title."

"So don't vote for him in the next election," Vaughn said sarcastically.

Marianna's body tensed and she got right in Vaughn's face. "This is not a joke," she said, her breath hot against his skin. "You think everything is so simple? So black and white? His rich friends will get him elected again, and the country will only fall further and further into ruin. You think democratic elections are actually democratic? You have a lot to learn, Michael Vaughn."

Emilio laughed and walked up behind Marianna, placing his hands on her shoulders. "I've taught her well, haven't I?" he said proudly.

These people are nuts, Vaughn realized, replaying Marianna's words in his mind. No wonder he'd been so snowed by her. Crazy people always made the best actors.

When Marianna turned to face Vaughn again, she looked like herself once more. Her face was sweet and girlish and kind. Vaughn's heart constricted as she reached out to touch his face. He tried to pull away, but there was only so far he could go. Her soft fingers finally cupped his cheek and she looked into his eyes.

"Thank you for my time in New York, Michael," she said softly. "These may have been my last few days, and I'm glad I got to spend them with you."

"It's almost over." Vaughn heard her voice in his mind. Those were the words she'd said at Wollman Rink that afternoon. He'd thought she meant that her trip was almost over, but she had been talking about her life. She knew that if she murdered her father, there was a good chance she would not live.

And her big brother, the heart and soul of La Rappresaglia, was just going to let her do it. He was going to let Marianna take the fall and most likely take a bullet as well.

"He doesn't care about you, Marianna," Vaughn said, his voice thick. "He's just setting you up—using you."

Emilio's face hardened, and Marianna shook her head. "You don't know what you're talking about."

"Think about it! He wants to punish your father. What better way than for him to see you, his beloved daughter, aiming a weapon at his head?"

Emilio stepped forward and punched Vaughn across his face, slamming into the same spot that the kidnapper had softened up two days before. Vaughn's head snapped to the side and his eye felt as if it were about to pop out of his skull, but he lifted his face and glared into Emilio's eyes.

"Do not attempt to poison my sister's heart," Emilio said.

"You're the one who's poisoned her," Vaughn spat back.

"Enough," Marianna said. "We have to go."

"You don't have to do this, Marianna," Vaughn said. "You have a choice."

Marianna's lips trembled slightly and her skin flushed. He gazed at her steadily, hoping to get through to her—hoping to make her see what she was really doing. For a moment he thought he had her.

"Marianna!" Emilio barked, seeming to sense the shift in the air.

Marianna blinked rapidly. "It's too bad we are on opposite sides, Michael," she said. "We could have really had something."

Heads bent together, Marianna and Emilio talked in low tones. Vaughn could tell from the intensity of their expressions that they were arguing over something—most likely trying to decide what to do with him. For a split second he almost hoped they would kill him so that he wouldn't have to face what was coming next—the tragedy, the humiliation, the shame.

That split second passed, however, as Vaughn told himself to focus. He had been trained to handle every situation. He had been trained to never give up. President Toscana wasn't dead yet. That meant there was still a chance. He had to stop thinking about himself and start thinking about his responsibilities—his duty to his country.

"We must go," Marianna said finally, turning to face him once more. She picked up a black evening bag and slung it over her shoulder.

"I would kill you, but there's no point," Emilio added matter-of-factly. "Whatever happens tonight, we are both turning ourselves in when it is over. I will stand by my sister like family should."

Vaughn didn't believe Emilio for a second. Maybe he was going to spare Vaughn's life now to keep his sister's trust, but he was not going to turn himself in. Vaughn could see the lie in his eyes. As soon as the president was dead, Emilio would disappear. Of course, he'd probably come back to the hotel first to murder Vaughn and tie up loose ends.

Marianna walked over to Vaughn and touched her lips to his. Nothing in him responded to her. He didn't close his eyes; he didn't move his lips. He felt nothing but revulsion.

"Goodbye, Vaughn," Marianna said, pulling away, for the first time addressing him with his last name.

Emilio turned the lock on the doorknob and held the door open for Marianna.

"Don't do this, Marianna," Vaughn said calmly, firmly. "They'll kill you. If you do this, you're dead."

Marianna paused in the doorway and cast one final, unreadable glance back at Vaughn. He yanked at his handcuffs, succeeding in nothing but knocking a few washcloths off the shelves.

But it was too late. The door was already swinging closed, and with a click that sounded morbidly final, Vaughn was left alone.

His mission had failed, he'd been duped, and now there was a very good chance that the president of Italy was going to die in front of the entire UN on United States soil.

13

VAUGHN BRACED HIS FEET against the floor, tightened every last muscle in his arms, and pulled with all his might. He strained against the pain of the metal cutting into his wrists, holding his breath until he thought his lungs were going to burst and all the tendons in his body were going to tear. Nothing happened.

The cuffs were unbreakable, the shelving sturdy. He relaxed his body and collapsed forward into the side of the shelf, resting his forehead against his elbow. As he gasped for breath, he thought about calling for help, but it was pointless.

The noise generated by the machines would drown him out. Until some hotel worker decided to come in and check on the laundry, he was stuck. By the time anyone showed up, he was sure it would be too late.

"Come on. Think!" he told himself through his teeth. He looked around the room for anything that might inspire an idea, but there was nothing. Nothing but towels and sheets and detergent.

Okay, I don't need to get out of the cuffs, I just need to get out of this room, Vaughn thought. Emilio had locked the door from the inside—the only lock the door had. That would prevent anyone from getting *in* easily, but Vaughn should be able to walk right out. All he had to do was figure out a way to Houdini himself out of his handcuffs.

If I could just break this side piece off, I'd be golden, Vaughn thought. If he could somehow detach the corner pole from the shelves, he could slide the cuffs free from the pole and escape. His hands would still be linked together, but that was an easy fix. Chloe had a handcuff key back upstairs at HQ, as did the dozens of cops patrolling the street outside the hotel. He yanked at his cuffs again to see if he could even rattle the two-inch-thick bar he was cuffed to, but it didn't budge. Still, he knew it wasn't unbreakable. Nothing was.

He needed leverage. Something to pry it off with. Unfortunately tools were not an option. Vaughn was just starting to feel helpless when he was hit with an idea. Gravity. Gravity was good.

Vaughn crouched to the ground, his arms above him, and reached out with his leg, kicking heavy bottles of detergent and bleach and fabric softener off the bottom two shelves. Bottles rolled across the floor and piled up under the table across the room. Once the base was cleared off, he strained to knock the boxes off the third shelf, jumping up and kicking out with his legs. It was slow going. Controlling his jumps and kicks was difficult with his arms tied together in one place, but eventually the boxes tumbled to the ground, spilling smaller boxes of fabric-softener sheets and stain removers.

Once the shelves were clear, Vaughn leaned back to catch his breath, gazing toward the top of the shelves. They were still packed with towels and sheets, but that was fine. He was going to need a little weight up top for his plan to work. Vaughn took a deep breath, braced his feet again, and pulled, letting out a groan against the effort. The shelves shimmied slightly, and Vaughn's heart leaped. A sheen of sweat formed over his skin and his wrists screamed with pain, but he ignored it all and sent every ounce of his strength to his arms.

Finally something gave. There was a loud screeching sound and the shelving started to fall forward. Vaughn jumped to the side at the last moment, and the heavy metal shelving smashed down, slamming into the side of the table. The sheer volume of the crash was surprising even though he had known it was coming. Vaughn was yanked to the ground, and he closed his eyes for a split second, praying his plan had worked.

When he stood up again, he saw mass destruction. The shelves were a mess, and clean white linens were piled everywhere, hanging from the top shelf and flung across the room. Just as Vaughn had predicted, the side pole that he was tethered to had been ripped free from the shelves, having hit the corner of the table at a perfect angle to pop the screws loose.

Vaughn slipped his cuffs along the pole until he was at the top of the shelf, which was jutting out at an angle toward the ceiling. He yanked his arms free, grasped the doorknob with both hands, and ran.

The basement of the hotel was a deserted labyrinth of concrete walls and flickering fluorescent lights. Dark corridors split and turned and opened up onto the dead ends of boiler rooms and electrical fuse boards. With each wrong turn,

Vaughn's tension level rose—each second was another second in which Marianna had succeeded and Vaughn had failed.

Finally, Vaughn heard voices, and he took a left, bursting into a long white room that served as an employee cafeteria. A few workers looked up from their trays, startled, and Vaughn saw them noticing his handcuffs.

"I need an elevator," he said, just hoping they wouldn't ask for an explanation.

"Uh . . . go back the way you came . . . make a right at the end of the hall . . . then the next right," a woman in a maid's uniform told him, rising slightly from her chair.

"Thank you," Vaughn told her before tearing out again. He found the service elevators easily and debated for a split second before hitting the button marked L for lobby. He didn't have time to go up to HQ and fill Chloe in on everything. Marianna already had a good head start. He had to get to the UN.

Vaughn jumped out of the elevator into a hallway off the lobby and headed for the front door. He caught the startled stares of a few people as he traversed the gilded, gleaming entrance hall, but he just kept moving. Out on the street, he jogged right over to the nearest police car and pounded on the window.

The female officer behind the wheel started, then rolled down her window.

"What do you think you're doing?" she demanded.

Vaughn held up his cuffed hands for her to see. "I need your key," he said.

Not surprisingly, the officer stepped out of the car and pointed her gun directly at Vaughn. He held his hands up in front of his face and looked her in the eye.

"Listen to me. I am a federal agent, I was kidnapped, and I broke free," Vaughn said quickly. "I will get up against your car so you can check my back pocket for my ID."

"Damn straight you'll get up against the car," she said, waving her gun toward the hood.

Vaughn stepped over, spread his legs slightly, and leaned his elbows on the car's warm hood. The officer slipped his wallet from his pocket and flipped it open.

"I'm CIA Officer Michael Vaughn. I was assigned to protect Marianna Toscana, but she . . . got away from me," Vaughn said, trying to keep it as simple as possible. "I need you to uncuff me and let me borrow your vehicle so I can get to the UN. There's an assassination attempt in progress, and I'm the only one who can stop it."

"I don't know," the officer said, hesitating. She looked fairly young and was probably just out of the academy. Vaughn could sympathize with the fact that she didn't want to do anything wrong, but he couldn't sit here and coddle her either.

"Look, Officer, you have a choice," Vaughn said. "You either help me and end up with a commendation when I tell everyone how I couldn't have saved the day without you, or you *don't* help me and a very important man dies."

Vaughn looked over her shoulder as she holstered her weapon and took out her key. He turned and held his hands out for her so she could work the lock.

"Thank you," he said, rubbing his wrists when the cuffs fell free. "Now I need you to do me one more favor. . . ."

* * *

Vaughn jumped out of the police car in front of the UN, clutching his wallet, and ran up the steps, past loitering limo drivers, security guards, and camera-toting reporters. The instant he was through the door to the brightly lit building, five tuxedoed men descended upon him, out for blood. In his casual sweater and pants, along with the throbbing welt on his face from Emilio's punch, he didn't exactly look like he belonged at a UN banquet.

"Where do you think you're going, sir?" a man the size of a tank asked Vaughn while others gathered around him.

Vaughn raised his hands in a gesture of surrender, holding his CIA badge up in front of him. "CIA. Official business."

"Uh-huh," Tank Man said, leaning forward to check his ID. "What kind of official business?"

Vaughn clenched his teeth as he heard a round of applause explode from inside the banquet hall. He was so close. All he had to do was get in there and get Marianna out before she did anything. The police officer who had uncuffed him had undoubtedly alerted Chloe by now, telling her about Marianna and the identity of the ponytailed suspect, so backup was on the way. Unfortunately Vaughn didn't have time to wait for it. He glanced at Tank Man and his stony expression. Vaughn was not supposed to divulge his mission to anyone outside the CIA, but time was of the essence here. He had no choice.

"I was assigned to protect Marianna Toscana because there have been threats on her father's life," Vaughn told him. "Tonight I found out that the assassin is going to be here, at the banquet. I have to get into that ballroom now."

"I'm sorry, sir. Until you pass through the security checks, I can't let you in," the man said, folding his hands in front of him and widening his stance as if he was going to grab Vaughn if he tried to bolt by. "Even the CIA has to comply with that."

Vaughn's nostrils flared slightly as he stared the man down. "Fine, then at least go tell Toscana's security people to keep him away from the podium. He'll be too exposed out there. Tell them Agent Vaughn sent you. They know me."

Tank Man eyed Vaughn for a second, deciding whether to believe him, and Vaughn glared back, just daring him not to take him seriously. Finally the man nodded tersely and jumped into action.

"All right, Bobby, take the agent to security checkpoint A," Tank Man said to the smaller guy over Vaughn's left shoulder. "I'll be right back."

Vaughn was escorted to a set of metal detectors, which he passed through with no problem since Marianna and her brother had relieved him of his weapon. A woman behind a low desk checked his ID against her computerized list of expected attendees and quickly found his name. Bobby shot Vaughn a chagrined look when he saw that Vaughn was supposed to have complete access to all areas of the building.

"Is Marianna Toscana inside?" Vaughn asked the woman.

She hit a few buttons on her computer and scanned the screen. "Yes sir," she said, nodding. "She arrived at seven-fifteen."

Vaughn clenched his fists to keep from lashing out. It wasn't this woman's fault that Marianna had been able to smuggle her weapon through security. Lacing into her wouldn't solve anything. But when he got back to Langley, he was going to tell whoever would listen that the security at the UN had to be dealt with.

"So, total clearance," Bobby said with an embarrassed little laugh. "I guess you can go in, then."

A sizzle of adrenaline shot through Vaughn. He whipped off his sweater and tossed it aside, looking Bobby up and down. He was a little bit broader and pudgier than Vaughn, but it would have to do.

"What?" Bobby asked warily.

"I need your jacket," Vaughn said. "I can't go in there like this—I'll draw too much attention."

"Right," Bobby said. Suddenly he seemed to grasp that there was something big going on here and he'd just been asked to be part of the solution. Vaughn could sense his rush of excitement as he slid out of his tuxedo jacket. He handed it to Vaughn, who pulled it on over his white T-shirt and black chinos. It was hardly perfect, but it was good enough to go unnoticed.

"I need your piece too," Vaughn said, holding out his hand.

Bobby looked down at the sleek silver gun in his shoulder holster, his eyes wide. "I can't relinquish my gun, sir."

At that moment, Tank Man appeared from around the corner, followed by Agent Roscoe, who was pulling at the collar of an ill-fitting tuxedo shirt. Tank Man's cold demeanor had shifted, and he now looked mightily disturbed, as if he'd just been told he and his team had let an armed assassin into a meeting of world leaders.

"Bobby, relinquish your weapon to the man," Tank Man said.

"What's going on?" Vaughn asked as he shoved the gun into the back of his waistband.

"Toscana refused to stand down," Roscoe explained, catching his breath. "He said he wouldn't be deterred by terrorists. He said he trusted that the CIA would take care of things."

"Damn," Vaughn muttered. He was all for standing tall in the face of threats, but Toscana had no idea what he was dealing with. He looked at Roscoe, his expression grim. "The assassin is inside."

Roscoe blanched, and Vaughn could see his

Adam's apple moving as he attempted to swallow. "Who is it?"

"It's Marianna Toscana."

There was a split second of silence as a pall of dread fell over the small group of men. Then, inside the ballroom, the audience erupted in cheers and applause once again. Toscana had just been announced. Time was running out.

"Vaughn!"

He turned to find Chloe running into the lobby, followed by a team of agents.

"Officer Rodriguez told me everything," she said.

"You have the photos of Emilio?" Vaughn asked.

An older agent stepped forward and handed him a small stack of photos—copies of the shot from outside the car dealership. Vaughn quickly handed them out to the security men and the other agents.

"He just cut his hair, so forget the ponytail," Vaughn said. "The best identifying mark is the small, X-shaped scar on the left side of his chin. He's here somewhere. Find him."

The agents fanned out, heading for separate entrances to the ballroom and various other points throughout the building. Vaughn looked down at Chloe.

"I'm going after Marianna," he said.

"Be careful," she told him.

"She's at table ten with her mother," Roscoe informed Vaughn. "They're right in the center of the room, two tables back from the dais."

Vaughn took a deep breath, and Bobby opened the door to the ballroom for him. He stepped inside to a different world. The ballroom chandeliers were turned low, creating a dim yellow glow in the huge chamber. On each table flickered tall candles surrounded by an abundance of fresh flowers.

Moving slowly, carefully, Vaughn wound his way around tables and chairs, passing by countless women in couture ball gowns and men in designer tuxedoes. Silver clinked against china, and guests whispered in hushed tones here and there as he headed for the front of the room. He watched Toscana delivering his speech from behind the podium—a dynamic orator, he had the room riveted. Vaughn respected the man, but he wished he had just agreed to stay behind the scenes for the night.

Doors on either side of the room opened, and Vaughn saw agents entering unobtrusively, keeping to the walls. They were checking the room for

Emilio. Vaughn hoped the man wasn't anywhere near the ballroom. If he did succeed in stopping Marianna, there was a good chance Emilio would snap and try to finish the job himself.

Up ahead, Vaughn caught sight of Marianna's back—her full head of soft curls. She sat in her chair, turned toward the stage, watching her father like the good daughter she was always pretending to be. Her mother sat across the table from her between two unfamiliar men, smiling up at her husband.

Don't turn around, Vaughn willed silently as he stepped within twelve feet, ten feet. *Just don't turn around.*

If Marianna saw him coming, it was all over.

Then, just as Vaughn was slipping around the last table that separated him from his mark, he saw Marianna shift in her seat—saw her reaching for her weapon. His heart flew into his throat and he stumbled between two chairs, jostling an older woman and causing a slight commotion. A few people noticed Vaughn and grew alarmed, but he didn't stop. Marianna was starting to stand. She was drawing her weapon. Vaughn was too far away to stop her. He did the only thing he could possibly do.

"Gun!" he shouted. "She has a gun!"

Screams erupted from around the ballroom. China crashed; glasses were knocked over. Vaughn saw Toscana look down into the audience and spot his daughter. He saw the man's eyes widen in terror and shock as he took in the small weapon now aimed directly at his head.

Toscana gasped. "Marianna?"

Vaughn threw himself over the last few feet, and just as he tackled Marianna to the floor, he heard the gun go off. There was an explosion overhead, and sparks sizzled and popped, showering down from above. Vaughn landed on top of Marianna, hard, as feet stampeded all around them, thousands of petrified people heading for the doors. Vaughn pinned Marianna to the marble floor with his knee. Beneath him, she started to cry.

"Did I get him?" she asked, turning her head to the side. A trickle of blood slipped from her nose as she coughed through her tears. "Is he dead?"

Vaughn looked up at the dais and saw Agent Roscoe helping a shaky President Toscana to his feet. Marianna's mother stood nearby, her hand to her throat, staring down at her daughter, at the gun that had flown from her grasp and lay a few feet away in the middle of the floor.

"No," Vaughn told Marianna. "Your shot hit the chandelier."

Suddenly Marianna's sobs grew severe, racking her body as she gasped for breath. Vaughn hauled her to her feet and she hung her head, turning her face away from her gaping mother. Chloe appeared at his side with a pair of handcuffs, which he quickly secured around Marianna's wrists. Her parents watched, dumbfounded, as Vaughn and Chloe led their daughter away.

Marianna cried all the way through the ballroom and lobby, down the steps, and into the car. Vaughn tried not to let himself be taken in—tried not to let his heart go out to her. As he stood on the curb and closed the door to the police car, locking her into the backseat, she looked up at him through her watery eyes. He had thought that he knew her so well, but in that moment he realized he had no idea what she was thinking. He never knew if her tears were inspired by relief that her father was still alive or frustration that her plan had been foiled.

14

VAUGHN SAT IN THE DEBRIEFING ROOM at Langley, wondering if he was ever going to stop feeling like a moron. Chloe stood next to him in front of her chair, giving Betty a rundown on everything they had found out in New York.

Marianna had been acting as the figurehead for La Rappresaglia while Emilio stayed behind the scenes. She had personally recruited several of her father's security personnel to the cause. She had engineered the kidnapping using four of her most incompetent men, knowing they would be caught and figuring it wouldn't be much of a loss—and threatening to kill their families if they breathed a word about her involvement.

Thankfully Chloe left out Vaughn's confessions about the Saturday night date and the kiss. She left out the clinging Marianna had done on the street and the fact that Vaughn had held her. She left out all her suspicions about exactly how involved Vaughn's feelings for Marianna had become.

"Thank you, Agent Murphy," Betty said. Chloe tucked her skirt under her legs and sat down, glancing hopefully at Vaughn. Maybe everything hadn't gone so smoothly in New York, but they had ultimately stopped the assassination, caught one of the top two people in La Rappresaglia and four of her men, and come home alive and well. All in all, it was a success. Now they just had to hope that Betty would see it that way.

"And now for the loose ends," Betty said, sitting forward.

Vaughn's heart sank, and he could feel Chloe tense up beside him as Betty opened a folder in front of her. She examined its contents over the top of her glasses, then sat back.

"Emilio Moreno is still at large," she said. "And Ms. Toscana is denying that he exists. We have photographic proof that there is a man out there who looks like he may be related to the Toscana family, but nothing else. The president himself is not talking."

"I don't believe it," Vaughn said. "So he's just disappeared? We have nothing to go on to find him?"

"Precisely," Betty replied. "Dominic Rizzio, your original prime suspect, has been cleared of all charges."

Vaughn and Chloe exchanged a look, and Vaughn felt his stomach hollow out. "I don't understand. We saw him attempting to purchase weapons on the black market."

"Yes, and his story checked out," Betty told him. She sifted through a few papers and found the one she was looking for. "He was purchasing weapons to arm the president's men. The money was released to him by Mr. Ricco Padua, the head of domestic security."

"But the president didn't say—"

"The president didn't know about the money or the planned transaction," Betty told him. "Apparently Mr. Rizzio was as shocked as you were when he found out his fellow bodyguards were members of La Rappresaglia."

Vaughn thought back to his interrogation of Dominic—his paling when he saw the photographs of the men they'd captured. So he hadn't been upset because they had caught his cohorts, he had been upset because his friends had turned out to be traitors.

Vaughn rubbed his forehead between his thumb and fingers. Apparently he wasn't going to stop feeling like a moron anytime soon. He was going to just keep feeling worse and worse.

"What about the woman? The one from the weapons deal," Chloe put in. "She thought Dominic was La Rappresaglia, too."

"Yes, but we don't know who she was or who sent her," Betty pointed out. "Whoever she was, she was misled. Dominic is clean."

Vaughn took a deep breath, processing what he'd heard. That young woman had come to stop Dominic from buying weapons to protect his president. Had she known she was stopping one of the good guys, or had she somehow been tricked into thinking she was stopping one of the bad guys? *Guess I'll never know.*

There was a knock at the door, and Barry and Elena walked in, each in their uniform black turtlenecks and slick ponytails. "Sorry to interrupt, but I thought you might want to see this," Barry said.

He walked over to the television at the front of the room and turned it on, flipping quickly through the channels until he came to one of the news stations.

Vaughn's heart skipped a beat the moment he saw the scene on the large screen. Marianna was standing behind a low wooden table in a jam-packed courtroom. The camera work was shaky, and the little red icon in the corner read LIVE.

"What is this?" Chloe asked.

"She's being arraigned today," Elena explained, taking a seat next to Betty.

Vaughn stared at Marianna's face, defiant and composed, her chin lifted, her eyes steady. The judge read the charges against her in Italian, and English subtitles scrolled across the bottom of the screen.

"You have been accused of treason, of an attempt to assassinate the president of Italy, of conspiracy to commit murder, of grand theft and destruction of public property. Ms. Toscana, how do you plead to these charges?"

Flashbulbs popped all around Marianna, filling the otherwise still and silent room. Vaughn found himself holding his breath, his eyes trained on the small girl in the center off all that humanity.

"Colpevole," came the answer.

Vaughn went numb. A collective gasp went up from the crowd, followed by the scraping of chairs and murmurs of surprised conversation. One word scrolled across the bottom of the screen: *GUILTY.*

Everyone in the room turned to look at Vaughn. He avoided their gazes by staring down at the table, trying not to dwell on anything that had happened over the past week. If he thought about it, if he thought about her, he might very well crack.

"Well, that's enough of that," Chloe said, grabbing the remote and muting the TV.

"Yes, I agree," Betty said. "I think it's time for the good news, don't you?"

Vaughn's ears perked up at her words, and Barry joined them all at the table. Betty's mouth twitched at the corners as she looked at the four of them.

"You should know that the Italian government has sent a letter of commendation to the White House listing all of your names and thanking you for bringing Marianna Toscana to justice," Betty told them. "Our esteemed director is coming down here this afternoon to congratulate you all himself."

Vaughn caught the gleeful grin between Barry and Elena and saw Chloe shift in her seat as she tried not to react in kind. Vaughn forced a smile. He was, as always, happy to be recognized for a job well done, but this particular victory was bittersweet.

He watched the silent television as Marianna was flanked by military police and her hands cuffed behind her back. He watched as she was led off past a crowd of jeering citizens, finally ducking her head away from their shouts. Vaughn's heart was suddenly impossibly heavy.

Marianna Toscana had been right that night back at the Plaza. She was the bad guy. And Vaughn had brought her to justice. He had done his job.

But Vaughn knew that he had also learned a very important lesson. Romance and the spy game did not mix. It was too complicated, too dangerous, too heartbreaking. If there was one thing he knew for sure in the convoluted, confused mess of his mind at that moment, it was this: Michael Vaughn would never fall for a woman on the job again.

Never.